WE
THE
PRETTY
STARS

WE THE PRETTY STARS

COURT HIGH: BOOK FOUR

EDEN O'NEILL

PROLOGUE
LAST SUMMER

Royal

"Royal, it's your dad. Calling *me* this time."

Probably because I'd been ignoring him. I waved Knight off, folding my arms as I leaned back against my Audi. My dad had been bugging me like crazy all day, which was normal for him when he got on a trip. I tipped my chin over at Knight. "Tell him I'm busy."

Hushed tones beside me on the phone, my friend whispering into the device. After a few moments, Knight shoved the phone in his pocket and came over.

"You tell him?" I asked, studying my boots. I was busy, extremely. I looked up to find a scowling Knight Reed, the blades of his dark hair sweeping forward when he forced his hand through them.

"He says we all better be at Windsor House in the next hour or he's sending the artillery," he said, and not looking happy about it. He crossed his buff arms. "My grandpa's with him. Some Court stuff we gotta do."

There was always some Court stuff, some Court events,

and I didn't give a shit about any of it. I hadn't for a long time.

Try telling my father that.

It was his legacy, the only thing he had that connected us and put me on a path toward something he found acceptable about me. It pissed me off, which was why I tried to shun my legacy as much as I possibly could. Especially recently with the closer we got to high school graduation. I wouldn't hesitate to put both him and this town in my rearview mirror, the place and him a reminder of what my father saw me as...

The one who ruined our family.

The guilt of that weighing on me even now, I pushed off my car, LJ and Jax shifting on their feet beside me. They'd been watching on when Knight got his call. All our phones had rung, but the difference was Knight hadn't ignored his. He had a good relationship with the Court, his grandpa and everything, so if my dad, one of the senior members, called him, he answered. He answered to the Court because he wanted to, not because he had to.

With that, LJ came over, pushing a hand to my shoulder. The guy sighed. "Probably for the best, man," he said, sweeping long blond locks over his shoulder when he turned. "She has to do this on her own."

She was in the distance, our friend. Paige had been standing out in the middle of the field for a while, her vantage point the Route 80 train tracks. She'd called us out here, completely in hysterics, and when she explained what she wanted to do, *I* went into hysterics. I admit I lost it, left the conversation.

There was another way...

She didn't seem to feel that way. She believed this, and the Court was the only way. I wouldn't lie. I always wanted Paige to join us. I had always wanted her to be a part of Court and that bond that united the other guys and me. That'd been when we were kids, though. It'd been before all the constant obligations and phoniness of the brotherhood. There was a lot of power in our ranks, a lot of dark deeds and corruption we constantly had to ignore. A drugged-out prostitute found in a random bedroom at Windsor House? One covered it up, couldn't be a thing. Word of one of our dads or uncles fucking around with someone at the office behind their spouse's back? Definitely didn't make a note of it. We couldn't, repercussions too severe. That's how things always were, and with that, more power than any man *or* woman should have. Being in the Court basically gave you permission to ruin someone's life. A guy got to play God while being a mere mortal, and something *I'd* been willing to do on my own for someone I cared about. I'd do whatever I had to do for that girl who was currently mad at me by those train tracks. The only problem? That girl never wanted to be saved. People didn't save Paige Lindquist.

She saved her fucking self.

I couldn't even watch the guys as they left me, heading over to Paige and what we ultimately had to allow her to do. The guys wanted to get all this out of the way, and though there was a process into the brotherhood, the end result was all the same. If Paige accepted the challenge of a haze now, it'd be under at least *our* control. We'd do it for her and with her. It'd be done, and then she could go through all the easy stuff later. She'd be one of us.

I braced my arms, forcing myself to approach. It was well into night, the headlights of my car guiding me and the others. It shined on Paige, her back to us all. Knight put a hand on her shoulder, and when he pulled her around, she pushed her arms around his big body.

"I'll be fine," I heard her say to him, myself lingering on in the distance. I couldn't quite go over there, not ready. What she was wanting to do was crazy and banned for a reason. So much could go wrong.

The sickness of my reservations I forced down as I

watched Knight step away, which allowed LJ in for his own hug. Paige actually lifted the motherfucker off his feet, a good head or two of height the guy had on her. She liked to show her strength, that she wasn't weak, but she didn't need to do things like that to prove her place with us. We knew who she was, stronger than all of us.

After putting LJ down, she grabbed Jax's basically buzzed head. He always had his hair shaved down so he didn't have to do anything with it, the lazy shit. She pulled him to her by the head, and after telling her to be safe, Jax let go of her. The guys came to me after that, pushing fists into my arms and giving Paige and me a moment. My friend stood before me in her jeans and a dark hoodie. It was the start of summer but it still could get terribly cold at night.

"You don't have to do this," I said, one final plea. "We can find another way."

We could find *another haze*, not one that had been banned by the brotherhood. Ramses Mallick's little bitch ass had let it get out that he'd been challenged with this haze, failed by denying this haze, and though I resented him at the time, he was right. Doing this could get someone hurt, even killed. It didn't matter these particular tracks rarely got used. That's why they'd been chosen for this haze, but still, shit could happen.

Instead of talking, Paige came over to me, and when she put out her arms, I grabbed her by the back of the neck, pulling her into me. She didn't get to be the guy on this one. She was going to let me.

"That's why I'm doing it, ass," she whispered, holding me close and smelling like candy. I always loved that, how she could smell so sweet but still be such a badass. She braced my back. "You know those assholes will never accept it if I do anything else."

Her doing the one haze that was banned amongst us would make a statement, get her acceptance. Not one woman had attempted to be a part of the brotherhood, and if she did this, her presence wouldn't be challenged. She was breaking the horse that couldn't be broken before and making us all look subservient to her because of it. Though she was right about what she said, that still didn't mean I had to like that truth.

"You'll call me," I said, pulling her away. "You'll call if you need anything. My dad's summoned us tonight, but I'll try to come back as soon as—"

"You won't." She put her hands on my chest, putting distance between us. Dark strands of her short haircut crossed her face, the wind breezing them over coal-black lashes. She pushed the hair away. "Because you can't. It has to just be me."

"It'll be whatever I want. *I* can be here." I could do whatever I wanted, my place high in our ranks. My dad owned half this fucking town. I could do whatever the fuck I wanted and would.

Paige shook her head. "I don't want you to be. *You can't.* I need to do this, Royal."

With every word, she was ripping me apart, and I turned away.

Paige grabbed me this time, pulling me in. A quick hug and she was pulling my head over into the line of her voice. "Now help me."

Help consisted of me getting her settled. She lay on the tracks, but when she pulled out the ropes, I hesitated again. This was a part of it. The haze had to be tied down to make it more of a challenge, but the whole thing made me sick.

Paige frowned. "Royal, please."

I'd do anything for this girl and she knew that, taking advantage of that. We were each other's everything, had been for so long. She was there through all the bruises, all of the pain of my father. In times I thought I'd give up, I didn't want to because she was there. She was there with her own problems, and I was there for her too. We were an unbreakable unit, bonded through so many hurdles. She knew I'd do anything for her because she would for me.

In the end, I tied those ropes around her wrists, binding her to the tracks, but I kept them so loose it was laughable.

"You tug these if you need to," I told her, the knots tied in a way so all she'd have to do to get up was move her wrists. "The knots are loose. You can get free easy."

And she wouldn't fight me on that no matter what she said. She was tied to the tracks. She was *bound*, and she could tell people that for the sake of the challenge.

Understanding, Paige let me have my way for once, smiling at me. Her chuckle was light. "Got it, and I'll be fine."

She better be, and after making sure she had her phone to call me, I did something rash. I took my own Court ring, pulled it right off my finger and put it on hers.

"This is yours now," I told her. "I'll get a new one. You're Court after you finish this. No one can contest that."

Her smile widened, and when the tears glassed her eyes, I almost broke down too. I had no idea why she was getting emotional, but because she never did, seeing it fucking did me in too.

Fighting it, I put a hand on her head, leaning down and kissing the top of her hair. She owed me one more thing before I left her, *a promise* and the only way I'd leave her.

"You'll tell me who it is after this," I stated, refusing to leave until she gave me her word. She'd kept certain informa-tion under lock and key from me, fearing I'd do something, and I probably would. I'd *destroy* the person who hurt her. I shook my head. "I want to know who hurt you."

Her chin lifted after I said that, her smile fading. My best friend wasn't without her own mistakes. She'd chosen to do certain things. She *chose* to sleep with a married woman but what she hadn't chosen was to be promised things, to be told she could have a life with this person, only to be toyed with for nearly a goddamn year. She led my friend on and told her there was hope for them. In the end, there never was hope, there was only *pain*, and I'd been there for the brunt of it.

"I promise," she said to me, a grit to her voice that had never been there before. This woman had broken her, destroyed her with her promises and bullshit. She had never planned to leave her husband. She had just wanted a young fuck, a trophy for her wall. It was nothing if not familiar in this town, my own father showing me that with all the pussy coming in and out of my house my whole life.

Touching my forehead to Paige's, I stayed there, hard-pressed to let her go. I could have gotten the revenge for her, gotten my brothers to destroy this woman's life, but Paige wouldn't let me act on her behalf. She wouldn't tell me who this bitch was on purpose because *she knew* things would get real ugly if she did. I'd do anything for this girl, truly, and though she definitely wouldn't admit it...

This haze was her saving me from that.

CHAPTER ONE

December

Two girls… Two teenage deaths in a matter of months.

What the hell is going on here?

I hadn't liked Mira. God, had I not liked her, but I never wanted her dead. I never wanted that, *for anyone* or anyone's family to feel what I'd felt over the passing months. I honestly hadn't believed it when we found out, that assembly the weirdest thing. They placed us all in the gym, Principal Hastings at the front with a microphone. He'd told us something, a student dead and…

The sheriff had been there too, Sheriff Ashford basically a mess standing next to our headmaster. At one point, he hadn't been able to hold it together and excused himself. After that, the headmaster continued, and though he didn't give too many details, he didn't have to in the end. Mira's story spread like wildfire in the halls of Windsor Preparatory Academy, word of her suicide lining the pages of the local paper. She'd hung herself. Right in her bedroom in the middle of the night.

What the fuck?

I hadn't slept at all that night, thoughts of Mira and whatever she was feeling replaying in my head. She'd threatened me not hours before that, threatened Royal, but she hadn't seemed sad. None of this made sense.

If confusion was my reaction, a chill was Royal and crew's. They wouldn't talk about any of it all, letting the conversations happen around them. At times, I caught the boys whispering to each other, leaving me out of things, and the day of Mira's funeral, Royal's vault of a demeanor was basically the same. He picked me up in his Audi, a stonewall aside from the affection he gave. Since we got back together, he hadn't allowed me out of his sight except to go home and sleep at night.

Even then sometimes he'd make it through my bedroom window.

Hershey always announced his presence, a soft yip, and after he petted her, he'd join me in bed. He'd hold me, not letting go. He didn't let go, not anymore. Even now on the way to the funeral, he had his fingers looped in mine while he drove, a lot going on in this car that wasn't being said. Though I didn't like that, I allowed it for the time being.

We were going to a funeral today.

The whole school was going, something I think was expected of the town. There wasn't even any debate that we'd all be going, this town. It was just what was going to happen, everyone coming. Birdie had texted me earlier that morning that she and a bunch of the basketball girls were going together. She'd invited me, but I told her I had a ride. Royal and I pulled up to a large white church with just the two of us, and when he left my hand, it was only for a few moments for him to let me out. Soon, we were united again on the other side of the car, entering a church together filled with so many people. I honestly think the whole town was there, pews upon pews of people, like this was a wedding.

Not yet another dark day.

This town seemed to keep having those, a cloud over this place's head. Blending in with the masses, I let Royal lead me to an open pew. It had a few people sitting on the end, but the majority of it was free. After taking off my coat, I sat down, and he joined, throwing an arm across my shoulders and smelling so good. I loved that heat about him, his warmth, as his green gaze circulated the crowd. He wore his blond hair pushed back and moussed, a stress lining his face I didn't like. Again, he was a vault. Albeit a beautiful one. He'd arrived at my house in a suit not much unlike the tux he'd worn when he took me to homecoming. It hugged his muscular arms and chiseled thighs in all the right places, the pewter tone a wonderful offset to his eyes. When I was with him, I felt protected and *usually* settled.

But not today. Today I watched him look anxious, a tension tugging dusky blond eyebrows together. I'd only leaned over to talk to him about that when several boulders masquerading as teenage boys arrived at our pew. Knight, Jax, and LJ had obviously driven to the church separately but they were here now. They each clasped Royal's hand one by one, an assembly line of acknowledgment. The pretty boys wore suits, looking like handsome men today, and after, they looked at me. I sat there, knowing I hadn't really associated with any of them since the initial assembly. School had been let out early that day due to Mira, and then had been the weekend.

Well, here we were now.

Royal and I were obviously a new development, and though we sat together at the assembly, there wasn't much talking then. At least to me.

Royal's arm lowered, and he moved his big body back to allow the boys to pass and sit. In my black dress, I wiggled back too, receiving a "hey" from LJ and nothing but a chin tip from Knight. That's just how Knight rolled, not ever much for

words. When Jax started to pass, he stopped. He made a
parting motion for LJ to shift his weight and make room as LJ
had sat next to me.

Rolling his eyes, the tall blond moved enough for Jax to
push his body into the space, and settled, Jax placed an arm
around me. This maneuver caused him to inadvertently touch
Royal's shoulder, which got Jax a swift growl on Royal's end
and a death stare that might scare me had it been directed
toward me.

"Sorry, man." Jax cleared his throat, returning his hand to
his lap. He gave me a little wave. "Hey, December."

It seemed things of the past had been forgotten, his aver-
sion to my relationship with Royal. I had a feeling that had to
do with things I'd been waiting to hear about from Royal's
end, but honestly, I wasn't mad at Jax anyway. Maybe I
should be, but a part of me really liked him, liked all of them
really. Even Knight. They did always look out for me, there
when I never really seemed to know I needed them. They all
played a place in my life due to connections with my sister.

I sat back, Royal's arm returning behind me. Squeezing, he
pulled me forward, and I noticed a silent exchange between
him and the guys. Even Knight had looked at him, nodding
before reaching forward and taking a program off the back of
the pew ahead. I had a lot of questions here, and they started
with that.

I tugged Royal's lapel. "What's going on?"

Lustrous green eyes shifted in my direction, a slight smile
to them before he cradled the back of my head. He brought
my head down, kissing the top.

"Nothing, princess," he said, *nothing* like I was stupid and
that he hadn't *just* promised me something not a few days
ago. He promised me information, that he'd let me in on
everything regarding my sister and what happened to her. He
said he'd put it out there and not keep anything from me
anymore. All that seemed to fall to the wayside after all this

with Mira, the road trip he promised me put on the back burner. I hadn't questioned it at the time. After all, the day of the assembly had been the day we'd planned to go. We didn't know when her funeral would be, so we stayed around for that. I hadn't forgotten though that he said he had to show me something, something he said couldn't just be told.

I hadn't forgotten a lot of things, my tongue held now only because my cell phone decided to buzz in that very moment. Ignoring it, I shoved it deep inside my purse, but that didn't stop the illumination.

Royal noticed.

Reaching across my lap, he slid his hand inside my purse, his proximity to the place he'd made me ache in the past too close. He retrieved the phone quickly and, after checking the face, held it out to me.

"It's Birdie," he said and, having handed me my phone, returned his arm to behind my neck. His eyes warmed. "Shouldn't make her wait, princess."

How easily he could distract with those eyes and he obviously knew it. I wouldn't question him in this moment, his fingers brushing the delicate hairs behind my neck, and considering where we were right now it was probably best. It wasn't appropriate, and *that* was the only reason I decided to read the texts from my friend, who was currently blowing up my phone with variations of the same message. She wanted to know where I was, if I was here and if so, where.

Birdie: We saved you a seat, toward the right side of the church if you're just coming in.

I gazed around the area, people standing up everywhere. This made it quite difficult to see anyone, but one thing I could see was the crowds were making an assembly line toward the front. When we had sat down, I hadn't really gotten a chance to see anything or anyone, but my eyes in that direction, I knew exactly why people were lining up.

She's up there.

Mira... Mira in a casket. She, herself, was still too far away but an ivory-colored casket with people bowing their heads over it could definitely be made out. She was up there for the world to see, obviously, since that's how these things worked.

I swallowed before gazing down back at my phone.

Me: I'm toward the back. Just got here.

Birdie: Oh, we're towards the front. Still don't see you.

Me: Just look for the Court brick wall.

Referring to Royal and his gang, I waited for the return text. It came swiftly.

Birdie: Whoa, what the fuck? Why are you sitting with Royal?

Two seconds later.

Birdie: Why is Royal's arm around you? Dude...

Truth be told, I hadn't seen Birdie and the others at the assembly either. The room had been really crowded, and after, they did let us out of school. Had I seen her, these questions might have come then since Royal and I had been very much together that day as well.

Me: Long story.

Birdie: Okay, give me the Cliff's Notes version.

About to do that, I was bumped when Royal got up. Soon, the others followed and before I knew it, I was being surrounded *literally* by a Court wall, tall boys even taller as they were standing up and I was sitting down.

Royal cradled his hand behind the back of my neck, kissing the top of my head again.

"We're going to go pay our respects," he said, pulling away. "Be right back."

He didn't let me argue. He didn't let me come. He only squeezed my hand before his boys followed him out of the pew, and that pissed me off.

I lifted my phone.

Me: We're seeing each other. Where are you guys?

Birdie: Front right. Three pews back and uh, what???

I gazed around, finding her and the others easily with their heights now that I had direction. That was definitely nice about having friends who played on the basketball team. Birdie with her big, brown bushy curls sat with her neck craned, waving an arm. After a moment, she nudged the shoulders of some of our other friends. The whole pew was basketball girls and boys, and Shakira sat right next to her. The dark-skinned girl with long braids also waved a hand, and Kiki, our other good friend, sat in the row behind them with more basketball players. The girl looked like a Korean model in her dress, which I knew her family originally hailed from as she'd told me. After Shakira reached back and pinched her, she waved too, her smile full.

I smiled as well before going back to my text message.

Me: Don't make a thing of it. It's still new.

Birdie: Okay, well. You'll explain after all this? I thought you were done with that.

He wasn't done with me, and I found myself with no desire at all to be freed. I loved Royal. I loved him so much, and though that honestly freaked me out, I'd rather lean into it than run away. He needed me, and I needed him.

Even if he didn't show that right now.

He'd made his way up to the front by this point, standing with LJ, Knight, and Jax. Like he said, they were paying their respects. Hands behind their backs, they stood gazing into the casket. I still couldn't really make out much besides that, Mira's body deep into the bed of the casket, but they had a picture of her right next to it. She was smiling. She was alive and wearing her cheerleader uniform. She was in the perfect peak of her life and not some shell just lying in a casket. She was complete. She was *whole*.

What the fuck is wrong with this town?

That question plagued me through a surprisingly short service. My mom had been Catholic so hers had been quite long. My sister's service was also a bit lengthy but mostly because of my dad. I hadn't seen him today, but hadn't expected him either. He'd been working a lot the past few days and had been gone the whole weekend entirely.

Fresh air couldn't have come at a better time upon leaving the church, and I drank it in the instant I was allowed it. Royal kept his long fingers laced with mine, and though the other boys were nearby, I felt disconnected from all of them. They kept looking at each other, *not* looking at me. They were doing more of their Court telepathy, and not only did that annoy me, I was insulted by it. Royal's hand left mine when we reached the street, but only because I got the distraction of other friends. Birdie and some of the basketball team made their appearance, and I gave Birdie a hug the minute she found me.

"This is all crazy, right?" she announced, looking quite sad really. All the girls did. We weren't Mira's biggest fans, but still, I didn't think anyone wanted anything bad to happen to her. Birdie swallowed. "I mean, I know she called me Big Bird, but I'd never want anything like this to happen."

She took the words right out of my mouth, and in the shuffle, I realized Royal, LJ, Knight, and Jax had allowed me to be led off. They currently stood in the street with a few other Court members, just talking. Royal's hands were in his pockets, and seeing me, he tipped his chin before going back to it.

I rubbed Birdie's shoulder. "Same. I didn't like her, but yeah. Never wanted this to happen."

"Any of you guys know why she did it?" Smoke pulled from Shakira's lips. She'd lit a joint right outside of the church.

Kiki smacked her hand. "Girl, you can't smoke that here, *now*."

"Girl, I can't *not* smoke this here. You saw that shit." Shakira shook her head, taking another drag. "Just tragic."

Agreeing, the joint got passed around. We made sure to do

it out of the fray and to the side of the church, but we were still technically on the front lawn. I didn't think any of us cared at that point, and even I took a hit, which got me a look from a few old people lingering outside. They should probably respect how others decided to deal with this stuff. I would if I saw them doing the same.

I folded my arms. "No idea why. But she didn't exactly seem like she had everything together."

In saying that, I thought about those last moments I'd had with her. She'd been seriously on one hundred when she freaked out on me and maybe wherever all that came from just got the best of her.

The joint made it over to Birdie. She tipped her chin. "You don't think it's because of you, right?"

Her saying that honestly left me gobsmacked. My jaw dropped. "What?"

"I just mean…" And in the next seconds, her gaze flitted over to Royal and crew. The guys were all still talking, in their own little world. I noticed not completely though. Royal and even Knight, Jax, and LJ were definitely keeping tabs on me. They were a part of their conversation with the other boys of the Court, yes, but their eyes definitely escaped in my direction quite a few times. As I was doing the same with them, I didn't make much of it. I needed to know where they were, and they obviously felt the same.

"Yeah." A finger came out, Kiki's, when she pointed toward my neck. "Is that his ring? We saw you sitting with Royal. At the assembly?"

"Mm-hmm, and Birdie tells us you guys are together?" Shakira's eyebrows rose. "*Is* that his ring around your neck?"

Having forgotten about the token, I placed my fingers to the very ring resting on my chest. Royal gave it to me the day we got back together, moments before everything changed once again.

"This doesn't mean you belong to me... It means you're a part of me, a part of all this. I don't own you because you can't be owned."

He'd said I couldn't be owned, but he was still owning me. I rubbed the ring. "Her taking her life can't be because of me."

Birdie shrugged, holding the weed out to Shakira. "We're not saying it *really* was, but you are with her man now."

"Okay, you guys are seriously overstepping. God—" I started to walk away, but was grabbed, Birdie.

She placed her hands on my shoulders, then pushed them around me, a strong hug. "We're sorry," she said, pulling away. "We're just trying to make sense of this. This is all super weird."

I agreed, very weird. Mira was angry, but she was also very sure of herself, both arrogant and confident. In a lot of ways, she was the yin to Royal's yang. She could have been the queen to his king, and that wasn't lost on me.

"Sorry again," Birdie said. I got another hug before the other girls joined in too. I was in the middle of a bear hug, the extended limbs of Amazon-sized women around me. The whole thing ultimately made me laugh, and I couldn't be mad at my friends anymore.

I embraced them. "I guess you're all forgiven," I said, getting some breath back in when they allowed me to pull away. Soon enough, the rest of the other basketball girls and guys joined us. I noticed very quickly a certain someone wasn't with them, and thinking back, I hadn't seen Ramses inside either.

"Ramses?" I asked the girls. They were all starting to get themselves together and leave, all deciding to go meet at a local diner to get something to eat instead of the stress of the burial. I think it was all just too much, too weird.

Birdie shoved her hands in her coat, the weather still a little chilly in the Midwest. "I didn't expect him today. Actually, I didn't even see him on assembly day. I texted him, but I guess his parents took him out of town."

Why hadn't I noticed? Clearly, a shitty friend. My new obsession with Royal Prinze had something to do with that, I was sure, and coming in for another hug, I told the girls I'd talk to them later. They left, and I got out my phone, trying to correct past wrongs.

Me: Hey, stranger. You all good? Didn't see you at the funeral. Mira's?

I hadn't seen him at the assembly either, obviously since he wasn't there. I just should have noticed.

God, you're so self-involved.

The bubble came up from Ramses's text, and as I waited, I noticed Royal, Jax, Knight, and LJ talking to Sheriff Ashford. I hadn't seen the sheriff since the assembly, but what's peculiar was, he was just as much of a mess now as he was that day. Royal himself was actually holding him up a little, the man crying. The sheriff had a fist over his mouth; from the looks of it, it was all he could do to keep himself together.

Ramses: Dude, I know. Crazy, right? Mira? And yeah, I'm good. I meant to text. Dad took me out of town. Some weird bonding thing.

I gazed away from the text as I watched another join the boys and Sheriff Ashford, Mr. Prinze. The middle-aged man looked like an older version of Royal himself, tall, dark, and maybe handsome if he didn't freak the shit out of me. He wore a black pea coat, relieving Royal when he reached a hand out and put it on the sheriff's back. He guided him away from Royal and his friends, talking quietly to the man. Eventually, Sheriff Ashford nodded his head and allowed himself to be detoured away. Heads together, Sheriff Ashford listened while Royal's dad talked, the pair putting distance between themselves and Royal and the other boys.

Me: Okay. Just keep in touch. This town is insane.

Ramses: Don't I know it. You check in too. I'll let you know when I'm back in town.

Pocketing my phone, I made my way over to Royal. The guys were still staring off at Sheriff Ashford and Royal's dad. Mr. Prinze had placed the man in a chauffeured car that pulled up right in front of the church. After, the man in the dark coat turned back, staring directly back at us.

Royal panned away then, the other guys narrowing their eyes. Mr. Prinze joined the sheriff in the back of the car, and as they cruised away, I shook my head.

"What was that about?" I asked, burying my hands deep in my own coat. I wouldn't miss these cold days, spring not able to come soon enough. We were seeing bouts of it, the weather not so cool, but everything was still dead around, no flowers. With almost no acknowledgment to what I said at all, Royal placed a hand behind my back. He started to guide us to walk away, but I wasn't fucking having that. I grabbed his down coat. "I asked you a question."

"Yeah, and if you'd give me a second to talk, I'd answer it." He passed things off with his signature cool smile, but that wasn't working on me. I was still pissed and didn't like being ignored. He pinched my chin. "It's nothing. I'm sure the man's just grieving."

"Grieving?"

He pulled me in when he guided another hand to my face. "Yeah," he said, but when I looked confused, he frowned. "You know, since the sheriff is Mira's dad?"

What the fuck? I *so* didn't know that. Not at all. "Uh, yeah. Didn't know that."

He blinked, this obviously surprising him. His hands settled at my neck. "Well, that's what that was about. He and my dad are friends. Dad's escorting him to the burial."

He and his dad were friends? *His dad* was friends with the very man who I believed helped cover up that my sister did a haze. It was a haze and a time I didn't understand. That was something *Royal* was supposed to help me with understanding.

He seemed not too hard-pressed to share all that now, starting to walk away, and I hit my wit's end.

"You told me something, Royal," I said, making him stop full stop. Right in the parking lot. All the boys did, LJ, Knight, and Jax. They turned, staring at me. My nostrils flared. "You told me you'd tell me everything. You told me you'd tell me the truth."

And he seemed not only to *not* want to do that now, but was passing it off.

I didn't understand.

What happened to what he said to me, how I couldn't be owned and we were going to do this together?

I stood up to him, and though he didn't look at me, I made him when I tugged on his jacket again. "You said you'd tell me everything."

His gaze hovered on me, the jump hard in his throat. Slowly, his sight veered over to his friends, but turning away, LJ, Jax, and Knight clearly weren't going to be a lifeline for him. They were leaving him to this as they should. This, what was going on here, was only between us.

Royal squeezed big hands over my shoulders. "Em…"

"Don't 'Em' me." I wiggled out of his hold. "The truth, *now.* Do you know why Mira took her life?"

He blanched. "Of course not."

"Why of course not?" I stepped up to him again. "You know she threatened me? Threatened you? She said she had something on you."

"Well, that had nothing to do with this. At least I think it didn't." He bunched a hand through sandy blond locks. "I don't know why she killed herself."

"But you do know a lot of things. A lot of things you're not telling me, but have no problem giving secret glances about to your boys."

Those friends here too, they shoved hands into their pockets. Both Jax and LJ turned away, Jax curiously silent. He was always the one to raise a voice about something. He was always the one to joke but apparently not today. He cleared his throat, and in those moments of silence, someone surprising stepped forward, Knight when he pushed a hand on Royal's shoulder.

"We can protect her better if she's a part of this," he edged, causing Royal's green eyes to close. "Come on, bro. You told us you were going to tell her everything too."

He had? Told them everything about us? So what had changed?

I saw that all over Royal's face, a torture haunting those emerald-colored eyes. He had a debate there, one that hadn't been there before when we were in his bed. It was there now.

He pushed out a breath. "It's going to take all night to get where we need to go," he said, his perfect jaw working. "So you're going to need to pack a bag."

CHAPTER
TWO

December

"December, why is Royal Prinze downstairs?"

Dad got back home before expected. He'd been gone since before the weekend, work. "And why does it look like you're packing?"

This had him moving inside my room, and when he closed the door I turned, the middle-aged man who was my father steaming from the tops of his ears. He'd been pretty laid-back since I had gotten home. Hadn't gotten on me about anything recently.

Perhaps, this had been too much, him seeing me pack. Because that's what I was doing, packing for a road trip. I shrugged a shoulder. "Maybe because I am? Packing?"

"And why would you be doing that?" He folded his arms, not even out of his suit yet. He must have seen Royal waiting on the couch for me and come right up here. He and Rosanna were down there, the woman not too pleased when I told her I was leaving too. The difference was she couldn't do anything about it. She wasn't my dad, and instead of arguing with me, she sat with Royal, the two sipping tea she'd made him right about now. My dad honed in on me. "Where are you going? You're leaving somewhere with him?"

I nodded, letting go of my stuff, and Hershey raised her head. She'd been watching me pack things into my duffel on the bed. I threaded a hand through my thick wavy hair. "Yeah, and we're going on a road trip." I couldn't give him more details than that because I didn't have any. I placed my hands on the bed. "We'll be back soon."

Dad visibly shifted red, his face filling up and everything. "You'll be back soon?" He threw a hand out. "And I, as your dad, am just supposed to be okay with that?"

He was going to have to be. I was eighteen and could do anything I wanted it. That decision ultimately might cause me to have to leave his house, but I was prepared for that. I had been before when he basically kicked me out of his life emotionally.

I took a pair of jeans from the bed and tucked them into my bag. My dad watched on, seemingly at a loss for words, but when I crossed in front of him to get to my dresser, he shook his head. "You're going out of town with that boy? I thought you were seeing the Mallick kid."

I cringed. I supposed dear ole Dad really was in tune with the social activities in town. I'd never told him I'd been "seeing" Ramses, but I guess the pair of us had been really good at fooling everyone. After Christmas break, Ramses and I had gotten into a fake relationship to spy on Royal and the Court, only for me to ultimately get information about my sister and the circumstances surrounding her death from Royal himself. I was about to get more of those answers, something this road trip would do. I pushed my sleeves up. "That's over."

"Over." Dad came around the bed, directing a finger at me. "Because of that."

I placed my hand over the necklace, the Court ring I knew to be there. It was a sign of what Royal and I were. Though I didn't want to get into all that with my dad, his accusations were true. I shrugged. "Maybe."

"Maybe," he'd parroted again, but this time his eyes were wild. His presence stopped me for a moment, his visible anger filling the room. His nostrils flared. "Out of all the boys in this town, *anyone*, you're doing this with him? The kid your sister got wrapped up with?"

So now, his true colors appeared. He'd acted so nonchalant in the past when Royal had been here, like he hadn't cared.

But of course he did. I saw that now and maybe just because of Royal's father. I knew Dad worked for him in some type of capacity and maybe a friendship between his boss's kid and me was fine, but this? Nah, this was too close to home. This was too close to Paige. I moved my jaw. "That's none of your business."

"Actually, it is my business. You're my daughter—"

"And now, you're taking ownership of that?" This frazzled him, his brow lifting. I huffed. "What happened to the dad who shoved me off on Aunt Celeste. Rosanna? Huh? What happened to him?"

Because he'd done that and to Aunt Celeste more than once. She herself had gone radio silent with me since I got back because she knew I was mad at her too. They'd both screwed me over, deserved each other.

Dad's perfectly styled hair tousled when he wrestled with it. "I'm not debating this with you. You're my daughter and you're going to unpack that bag right now." I continued to pack, and he pulled the bag. "I mean it, December. Now, quit acting like a child."

At this point, Hershey was between us, my chocolate Labrador retriever puppy. She was looking like a preteen puppy now more with her size, and she came over to me. I held her. "No offense, Dad, but I'm eighteen. I can do whatever I want and I have before. Now, you can take my stuff, *my bag*, but I'm still going."

"But why with him? Why have anything to do with—" He stopped, but not because of anything I did. He just stopped on his own. He dampened his lips. "I'm not okay with this. *Please*."

He'd never asked anything of me, at least not like this. He'd never said "please" before. Like it was a request and an option.

My bag slid from his hands. "I just want you to be okay. That's all I've ever wanted. Now, you're right. I can't stop you. But I want you to."

I watched that move across his eyes, eyes that had never failed to judge or discipline me. None of that was there now, only a father asking his daughter something. Because I couldn't abide by the request, I tugged my bag over, zipping it. "I'll be back soon."

My next move was to take Hershey. I packed some stuff for her too. I'd left her behind too much in the past and Royal said it'd be okay. I also had no resources I wanted to ask to take her. I was indebted to my dad's housekeeper, Rosanna, for a lifetime for not only taking Hershey in when I had no one else, but me as well.

I started to pick my pup up, but Dad approached.

He raised hands. "I can hold on to her. A dog wouldn't be good on the road."

He'd said this so nonchalantly, and though I'd seen him bond with Hershey rapidly over the passing months, I'd be hard-pressed to say him wanting to watch over her didn't come with an ulterior motive. If he had her, I'd have to come back. If he had her, I *would* come back, and he knew that.

I wetted my lips. "She needs to be feed and watered every day. Played with?" These things were obvious, but he was always gone, always working. I had hesitance I should even be putting out these instructions. I should take my puppy and say to hell with all this.

But then Hershey went over to Dad. She knew him and was letting him take her. He picked her up, rubbing her head. "I know. I had a dog as a boy."

That surprised me, very surprising about him. I supposed he was a kid once though. I picked up my bag, tossing it over my shoulder. My next move was to pet Hershey, which I did before leaving. I took the stairs in quick time, and Royal stood up the moment I came into the living room. Rosanna was there too, but she held back anything she wanted to say. She simply took Royal's and her dishes, her smile faint on me before removing herself from the room and the situation. I felt bad I was clearly causing her worry as well, not my intent. I was trying to do something after leaving this room, this town. I needed to know some things.

Those things all remained concealed with the person Rosanna left in this room, Royal when he approached my dad and me. He'd changed out of his suit, in a simple pair of jeans and a T-shirt that formed tight over his biceps and shoulders. We'd stopped at his house for some things too, and he rubbed his hands, staring over my shoulder at my dad. "Mr. Lindquist. Hello, sir."

Dad appeared at my side with my puppy in his arms. He placed Hershey down, and right away, she padded over to Royal. The large boy instantly dropped to a knee, always a fan of her. He made her do her dog smile when he ran his large hands all over her head and face. Her affection caused him to smile too, and he had such a nice one of those. He really didn't do that a lot, more pain I saw through his eyes than anything. He'd been through a lot, most of which I probably would never know. He kept a lot of himself away, even now after we'd gotten together.

Dad and I were silent, watching as Royal played with the

dog that always saw something in him. Hershey loved him, even before I knew I did.

Dad shoved his hands in his suit pockets. "So, December tells me you're going on some kind of road trip? You know it's a school night, Royal."

Royal rose, and coming to my side, he folded a hand behind my arm. "Yes, sir. I do. Trip shouldn't take very long. We're going to Corrington Meadows."

"Corrington Meadows?"

Dirty blond hair crossed over his eyes with his nod. "Yes. Going to pay our respects. For Paige, you know?"

I physically had to keep my breath from expelling. He hadn't told me we were going there, and honestly, at first listen, I hadn't made the connection.

We're going to pay our respects...

My sister had been found in Corrington Meadows. She'd been found there, and *that's* how all this began. All too soon, I felt Royal's hand brace my arm, tucking me back into him. He was holding me tight, keeping me close...

So obviously to keep me upright.

In his own daze, this went unnoticed by my dad, the man playing over the information himself behind his eyes. With this new info, I *just knew* he'd resist. He'd fight even more on top of his issues with Royal.

Dad dampened his lips, but broke out of his haze at a nudge to his shin. Hershey was trying to get his attention, nudging him. Getting on her hind legs, she pressed paws to his leg, and my dad hunkered down, picking her up. Dad's jaw tightened. "So if I make a call to the school... forty-eight hours would be good for a trip?"

I stared up, to his eyes. He was serious, and just as much as he stood there before us.

Removing his hand from my arm, Royal placed his together. "I believe that would be appropriate. If it takes any longer..."

"I'll text," I came in with.

Dad swallowed. "You'll call."

"I'll call." The least I could do with him being so cool about this, taking Hershey.

With a nod, Dad cleared the doorframe for us, and Royal, the gentleman he was, took my bag off my shoulder. He gave Hershey a little pat, and after I did too, the pair of us passed my dad. Dad followed us into the foyer, watching on as Royal opened the door for me.

"Make sure you take care of her, Royal."

Royal turned at the door, lifting his chin. "Will do, sir. I'll take real good care. I promise." Royal started to go but faced Dad again after stepping a foot outside. "That's a nice ride you have out there. Is it new?"

I hadn't noticed Dad pull up in anything different but when I gazed outside to the driveway a sparkling blue Aston Martin was parked next to Royal's sleek Audi. It must have been new. I'd never seen it.

Dad cradled Hershey. "It is new, but it's going back. It's a gift, but I'm not accepting it."

Must have been a good friend to give him something so nice. I faced Dad and noticed he exchanged a glanced with Royal, but Royal didn't give much acknowledgment to it. Instead, Royal asked me if I was ready, and since I was, I started to follow him out. Dad touched my arm, but before I could speak on that, he slid something out of his pocket and into the purse on my arm.

"For protection," he said. "Use it if you need to."

Royal had stopped at the base of the house's steps, but I didn't think he'd heard Dad. Royal was waiting there, idle with my bag in his hands, and I looked at my dad. "I'll be fine. You don't need to worry."

My words didn't do anything really to console him, and I saw that just as easily as the worry on his face. He was letting me go with this boy he didn't trust, but that didn't mean he liked it.

CHAPTER
THREE

December

"Your dad really cares about you."

I brought my gaze up from the pepper spray Dad had not so discretely put in my bag. I pulled it out. "I guess this means he cares."

This had Royal smiling, like seriously grinning. Reaching over, he threaded long fingers with mine. He kissed the back of my hand. "I promise not to give you a reason to use that."

I knew he wouldn't give me one, the only reason I showed him. I could take Royal Prinze, let him come at me, and I'd come right back. I had before.

Smiling a little myself, I put the pepper spray back in my purse. Settling in, I took Royal's hand and placed it with mine onto my lap, more at peace than I should be considering where we were going. I hadn't gone with my dad to identify my sister's body last fall. He'd done that all on his own.

"Why are we going there?" I asked. "Corrington Meadows? You didn't tell me that."

He played with my fingers as he navigated the road. We'd

been driving for a while, the world dark on a highway lined with cornfields on both sides. This was the beauty of living in the Midwest, natural landscape always around. He frowned at the road. "That's just where we have to go for this. What we're about to do."

"Which is?"

A tongue ran over his full lips. He faced me. "This isn't something I can really explain to you. I could but…" His gaze shifted to the road, his eyes creasing hard. "I think it's best we go there and you find out everything that way. Believe me. I wish we were going anywhere else."

The terror rising inside me, I sat up. "But why? Royal…"

Gold lashes flashed in my direction, and because he most likely saw the panic in my eyes, he kissed the back of my hand again. Without words, he let go and reached behind the seats, pulling out a blanket. After working it around me, he pushed an arm around my shoulders, bringing me into his chest while he drove.

"Just sleep, okay?" he requested, bringing me closer and kissing the top of my head. He gazed back on the road. "Give yourself just one more night, one more before everything changes."

How could everything change even more than it already had? The prospect of that embedded more fear, and lifting the arm rest, I settled in under Royal's arm. I'd try to sleep. But I had a feeling that wouldn't be any easier than anything else I had to deal with since coming to Maywood Heights.

———

"Dad says you're out of town?" Aunt Celeste referring to my dad as anything other than a phrase laced with disdain was new. She usually referred to my dad as "Rowan" or my father.

Turning in the hallway, I stared into the diner. Royal

stopped us for breakfast after a quick night in a motel. I'd pretty much woken up there, most likely carried, as eventually I had fallen asleep in the car.

The beautiful boy I traveled with currently sat at our table, drinking a cup of coffee and only that. He'd turned down food completely, pretty much just watching me eat.

Like he knew he was being thought about, Royal panned toward me, his smile small as he lifted a hand in my direction. He looked delicious in his T-shirt and jeans, always did.

I pushed hair behind my ear, putting my back to him. The call came to my phone after leaving the bathroom. "Yeah, we're in Corrington Meadows."

When my aunt called, I'd been surprised with my desire to pick up. Maybe I'd just needed some semblance of strength. I'd yet to know what I would be shown today.

"That's what he said," Aunt Celeste said, the clang and chatter of the diner full steam ahead. Corrington Meadows managed to be an even smaller town than Maywood Heights, nothing but small shops and farmland. It was like a mini version of the town I knew, even more sleepy. The diner was the busiest I'd seen the town at all since arriving here. Aunt C. breathed heavy into the phone. "Well, come back soon, safe. I plan to come into town and see you soon."

I stared at my worn Converse. "Yeah? Why?"

"Just to see you, love. I can't get there right away. Have to make some arrangements at work, but your dad told me any time is fine. He's agreed to put me up."

That sounded exactly like World War III in the making and nothing my dad would normally agree to. Maybe he was worried about me or something, how weird he'd been acting before I left…

I folded my arms. "I don't need you to do that."

"Have you ever thought and wondered that maybe the visit isn't for you but for me? God, December. I've lost your mom and your sister. Lost them way too soon."

The guilt raged inside, hammered within that I wasn't the only one in this world grieving. I'd been so mad at both her and my dad I hadn't thought to wonder about how she felt.

"I'm all alone out here, you know?" she continued. "I miss you and since I don't have a lot of time with you before whatever you decide to do after graduation… yeah, I'm coming to see you."

I figured she'd be all gung ho about wanting to start her life. That's why she'd wanted to shove me off on my father. I heard them both talking about it the day of my sister's funeral, both of them wanting to rid themselves of me. I shrugged. "I guess I thought you'd want the time on your own."

Silence on the other end, and I heard her sigh.

"If I'm being honest, I can't tell you what you heard that day," she stated and sounded like she was moving around the house. "I can't tell you what was said because I don't remember. There were a lot of emotions that day, and I'm sure I said things that—"

"Well, I remember, Aunt C." I shut my eyes, a whisper in my voice. I remembered what she said all too well. I remembered not being wanted and even more when I'd been forced to go out on my own. Another heavy breath. "I remember every word. That's why I left."

"I know, and I'm so sorry about that. I'm not perfect, December. I made a mistake, and I own up to that."

"Is that the reason you're coming over?" I asked, wiping a stupid tear. "Forgiveness?"

"Part of it, yeah. The other part is because I need you. You don't have to forgive me now, but at least let me be a part of your life again."

I supposed I could do that for her, telling her so, and I turned. Royal made eye contact with me again, and though I knew he wasn't rushing me, he was sitting by himself. His attention redirected when the waitress filled his coffee.

"I gotta go, Aunt C."

"Okay, but be careful. Your dad told my why you're there, and I hope whatever it is you need from your visit you get."

I hoped so too, starting to end the call before she spoke again.

"Oh, and I almost forgot," she said. "A couple of people came by to see your sister not that long ago. One of them was a boy? A young man? I only mention him because your sister didn't really have any friends here. Does he go to your school?"

"I don't know. What did he look like?"

"Blond and excuse me when I say this because I'm *well* into my forties, but gorgeous as hell. He reminded me of the guys from the boy bands I used to have on my walls as a kid."

Well, that sounded familiar. I panned again to find Royal. He was staring at me again, and after ending my call, I ventured over. He stood as I got there, his hand reaching for the back of my arm.

"Everything okay?" He moved hair out of my face, his fingers ghosting along my skin. I'd never get over how it felt to be touched my him. Never.

Nodding, I picked up my bag. "Aunt C. She was just checking in. She said someone came to see my sister in LA. A blond boy who looked like the boy band guys she used to have on her walls."

Smiling a little, Royal threaded his fingers in mine, making sure to give the tip directly to the waitress on the way out. I didn't see how much he gave her, but the wad of bills was easily bigger than my OJ, toast with peanut butter, and his coffee. He pushed the door open for me. "I'm flattered. Did you tell her it was me?"

"I told her I suspected a boy from school, yeah." We stopped on the sidewalk, and he grabbed my other hand. I studied his face. "Why did you go out there? When even?"

"After the fight," he sighed, then let go of my hand to scrub one through his perfect hair. It fell so hotly over his eyes I wanted to touch it and did. He smiled. "I just wanted to see her. Your sister has a way of opening my eyes to some things. Always."

"Did she that day?" I asked, and his gaze left, fell across the street. A car started to come by, and Royal waved for us to pass.

"She did," he stated once we crossed the street, and it took me a moment to realize where we were. Royal hadn't said where we'd be going today, but when I noticed the name on the building, I let go of his hand.

I stepped back, *way* back, and shook my head. Why were we outside this building...

Why were we at the Corrington Meadows's Coroner's Office?

CHAPTER
FOUR

December

"This is needed, December. I swear it is."

But how? And *how* could he make me come here? My sister's body had been in there… *her dead* body. I shook my head again. "What the fuck, Royal?"

He started to approach, but I lifted my hands. He frowned. "Em…"

"Don't *Em* me." This was too much, too *everything*, and what did being here have to do with the truth only he could give? Was he messing with me?

What the fuck?

I walked in the opposite direction, but Royal got to me before I even hit the street. He pulled me forward. "All the answers start here—"

"What answers?" I shook out of his grasp. "You've been a vault, and this is cruel."

"It may be, but it's necessary. What's inside is necessary." He sighed toward the heavens, shoving hands into his pockets. "You know what? You're right. This is too much. It's too much for you, and I never should have taken you here—"

"Don't do that. Don't act like I'm weak!"

"You're not, but, December, this would be a lot for anyone. Coming here?" He threw a hand behind his neck. "It would be for anyone. It was for me."

I blanched at the admittance, the fact he'd come here unknown to me.

Perhaps, he knew I had no idea, my surprise all over my face. Approaching, he pushed hands to the back of my arms, warming me through my coat. "I came here after you left for LA. That's why I wasn't at your sister's ceremony."

"Why would you come here instead of the service?"

A tongue dampened his full lips, and he reached up to brace my face. "Because I needed to know the truth about some stuff. A trail brought me here, and I followed. I fucking followed it and unleashed all kinds of fucking bullshit I never wanted you to be a part of."

Tears, actual tears, fell and streamed thickly down my face. Royal wiped them away, his thumbs running through those hot trails. By my cheeks, he brought me forward and pulled me directly into his hard chest.

"Baby, I never wanted you to be a part of this." So much emotion in his voice, the tone gravelly. Smoothing hands over my head, he kissed my hair in the cool breeze. "Just give me a reason. A reason to let you go and get you the fuck out of this place. It's your call, Em, and I'll do it. I'll do anything. I'd give anything to protect you from what I know."

I knew he would, and had in the past to the point of more cruelty. He'd rather hurt me to keep me away than tell me the truth, his MO.

I was starting to understand so much about this beautiful boy, the layers of his heart no doubt twisted and mutilated from previous pain. I was sure he'd experienced years of it, physical scars I'd seen. He did things the only way he knew how.

"I want to see," I gasped, gripping his arms. I buried my face into his jacket. "I want to know whatever it is you have to show me."

Despite what I said, Royal didn't move, the pair of us just standing there in the chill. I physically had to separate myself from him, his cheeks filled with red from the wind. I touched one. "I think I just need your help."

Nodding, Royal led me inside a building so sleepy in this AM. It was still early and we didn't even have to check in at the doors, just walked on in, and Royal had clearly been here before. He led the way, his hand tight in mine. A few times he kissed the back of it, then eventually brought his strong embrace around me entirely. He guided me down a hallway barren of people, brick walls painted white and air smelling too sterile. It was like they bathed the place in bleach, pungent and entirely too clean. Coming across a door, Royal stopped in front of it.

"Let me have your hands," he said, and I gave them to him. He pulled off my gloves, then his own with his teeth. After pocketing them both, he rubbed my hands in his, taking the moments to bring them to his mouth.

He breathed so much heat into them, his eyes closed and mine shut too. I stayed in the dream, allowed him to take me away. I realized in that moment I think that's why he did it. He was giving me more time…

Maybe even giving himself a few moments too.

Letting go, he touched our foreheads together. "You ready?"

There was no getting ready for something like this. Being here already had changed everything, but being brave, I told him I was, and after he let go, he knocked on the door behind us. Royal's fist touched a glass window lightly, opaque so I couldn't see inside.

The door opened only seconds later.

A man stood there, a thin man in a white jacket. He also wore rubber gloves, his name plate stating, Dr. Felton. Dr. Felton barely greeted us, a nod like he'd been expecting us. Stepping back, he allowed us entry into the space behind him, more of that antiseptic smell blasting its wave on me. The array forced a wave of nausea I didn't anticipate, and Royal grabbed my hand. He squeezed as if he knew, and after we got inside, Dr. Felton closed the door.

"I assume you have payment?" the doctor asked, and acknowledging that, Royal pulled out his wallet. He took out more bills, handing them over to Dr. Felton.

Royal replaced the wallet back into his jeans. "There's more in there for time and the room. We won't need you."

I blanched. He really had done this before.

The doctor pocketed his cash. "Very well. I'll get you what you need, then you have the space to do with as you please."

I followed him with my gaze as he rerouted to a book-shelf, and with his back turned, I finally got a moment to take in the room. The area appeared as an operating room, a metal board in the center with various tools on tables surrounding it. There were all kinds of operating devices, knives and blades...

She was in here.

The sickness rose again, and like wildfire, Royal returned. He placed a hand behind my arm this time, waiting while the doctor ventured over from a wall full of binders. Dr. Felton only had one when he returned.

"As always no pictures," he said, eyeing us. "The files in here are restricted."

"And your only copies?" Royal asked, his expression vacant, hard. I'd seen him like this enough times to know the legitimacy. He gave zero fucks if he expected something, not an act at all.

Dr. Felton nodded. "Yes. I preserved them after your last

visit. They won't be destroyed as previously requested. That is as long as payment continues?" Royal need only give this man a look, and he was placing the book on the metal table, his answer apparently given. Dr. Felton stepped back. "You have as long as you need."

The doctor left the room, and with his absence, I felt the chill, the reality of whatever this was before me. I was about to see something and I had a feeling it was something I didn't want to see. Royal came behind me, unzipping my coat but when he started to take it I shook my head. It may be warm in here, but I was so cold.

He put his hands on my shoulders. "I won't do anything. Not until you're ready." He was leaving this to me. All of this? I shook my head again, and he brought his arms around me, his chin brushing my ear. "What do you need from me, Em?"

I needed this; my eyes closed as I embraced the weight of his arms. "What page do I need to turn to?"

"One forty-two. Do you want me to do it? I can. Just give me the word."

I must have given him enough of one because soon, he was reaching around me. He opened that binder, and the appropriate page must have been marked because the book opened right to page 142. Getting to what Royal needed me to see was too easy.

So easy…

I covered my mouth at only a look of photos, hands that didn't look like hands. There were only pieces… fingers and the flash of a face, bruises on cheeks and around eyes…

I can't do this.

This wasn't her. This wasn't what she was supposed to be. This wasn't my sister. This wasn't…

"Em!"

I collapsed to the floor, and Royal came with me, holding me, squeezing me so damn tight.

"December, I'm sorry. Sorry," he rasped, pushing back my hair as he rocked me, but sorry for what? Showing me this? My sister's spare parts? What did this show? What could this possibly show?

"Why?" I ached, shuddering in his arms. "Why did you do this? Why would you show me this!"

"Because it's the truth." He ached too, his deep voice so thick and pained. "It's everything. Paige, she… Paige had bruises. Bruises around her wrists and forearms. Her neck…"

Her neck?

"It all shows signs of trauma," he continued. "Do you understand me?"

I didn't understand, and he pulled back my hair, clearing it from my ear when he leaned in.

"The bruises were everywhere, Em. Her waist and in between her legs…" Royal shook his head. "There's *trauma* everywhere—"

"What are you trying to say!" I turned around, and he let go of me. I'd never seen such torture on his face, such raw emotion, when he squeezed his eyes.

He dropped his hand. "I'm saying your sister was dragged by a train, yeah. But there's a binder full of evidence that shows she was dead before it even came down the track."

CHAPTER
FIVE

One year ago

Paige

"How are you holding up, Paige?"

I opened my eyes, unable to fucking breathe. Pressing my hand to the office's window, I stared outside. People were across the street in a park, people together and just chillin'. One couple pushed a baby in a stroller. They were together, not thinking about anyone else or fucking drama.

"Paige... I'm sorry. I just can't do this anymore. It's... It's not right."

"Paige?"

My lashes flashed, and I turned, my breath stolen away again. Lena stared at me, expectant. She told me to call her that. Not my counselor anymore since freshman year.

"What?" I asked, bracing my arms. She'd said something to me.

The woman's smile was slight, her eyes always warm as she lounged back against her desk. "I asked how you'd been holding up. You came to see me. Gosh, it's been years."

It had been years, enough for me to notice. I should have come to her sooner. I should have come to her before things got so deep.

But that's not why you're here now.

The reason was stupid, incredibly, and I realized that the moment Lena left her desk and approached. I couldn't look at her directly in the eye, so close to someone else's…

"I'm sorry." I really was dumb, and I left, needing to breathe. I needed to get out of there.

Why can't I just let go?

I didn't want to, anger and fury filling me. The betrayal was suffocating, my own damn fucking fault. I should have known that's where this would go. I wasn't worth it to anyone.

I wasn't worth fighting for.

Certain of that now, I passed Lena and forced myself to let go of a lifeline. I *needed* to let go, so obsessed I had to see Lena. She'd been my friend, but that's not why I came to her. I wanted something, selfish for needing only one last look of those eyes. They weren't mine to look at, to have. That fact had been proven to me, and I had to accept that.

"Paige, wait."

I clipped my old counselor's shoulder, Lena, on the way out. Me coming in here like I did, then leaving wasn't fair to her, but I didn't fucking care. There'd be no more hurt after I left this room, only pain.

There'd only be revenge.

I slammed the door to the downtown practice, leaving the building as quickly as I'd come. I was so happy I'd come to see Lena in the end. I'd needed a reality check.

I needed one last goodbye to those eyes.

CHAPTER SIX

The present

December

I drowned in a sea of images, reality I forced myself to take in.
I had to see the truth. I had to experience it, and doing so
ripped me apart, each and every image I forced myself to
thumb through. I had to see it all, though. I had to be *shown*
the truth, and sometimes, yeah, Royal had to turn those pages
for me. Sometimes, he even had to hold me up just for me *to
see* those images, but I was there for every one. I was there for
the story.

I was there for this new reality.

He showed me pain. He showed me trauma, and every
moment he made sure to remain stronger than me. He
soldiered on through my screams, held me through my terror,
and told me the story.

No matter how much it broke him too.

He told me there was tearing at one point, physical evidence of forced entry discovered via the autopsy. There were no photos of this, but Dr. Felton had left detailed notes, ones Royal talked about before he allowed me to read the notes myself. He'd been absolutely *shaking* when he told me about the evidence, and reading on, I understood why.

The vomit came right behind.

It came in a never-ending wave, Royal holding me the whole time while I let it out. I filled probably two trash cans, the *tearing* noted to be between my sister's legs when I made it that far in the notes.

Rape.

The letters had been big and red, a blur behind cloudy vision. I cried my goddamn eyes out, as much as I could between bouts of vomiting. Royal gripped me within his strong embrace, not letting go, and eventually, he decided I had enough. He told me my life would change just the day before, to get one last good sleep when we were on the road.

I'd never sleep whole again.

He had me on the road after we left the coroner's office but not for long. We checked into a hotel, but as far outside of Corrington Meadows as he could get me. It was a bigger town, a nicer city and hotel, and with more than just a bed and small bathroom like the motel he'd checked us into the night prior. We hadn't had many options in Corrington Meadows, but this new city he'd been able to get a suite. It had three rooms and a giant bathroom, and though I had no idea how much it cost, I had a feeling he spared no expense. Royal basically carried me into the suite at that point, no words shared between us since in Dr. Felton's office. They hadn't come from me, of course, all from him for so long...

"There was tearing between her legs, Em..."

I couldn't breathe again, dizzy, and Royal physically picked me up and secured me in his muscled arms. Like an unshakable mountain, he walked with me to the bathroom, only taking the moments to kick down the lid of the toilet before setting me on top of it. He helped me brush my teeth, then ran me a bath in a tub fit for like five people. Nothing but silence was between us as he gathered the bubbles up and made them nice and big. After he finished, he only left me for the moments it took to get me a change of clothes from my bag. He placed them down when he returned, and after confirming I'd be able to handle the rest, he left me in the bathroom. I sat there for so many moments before deciding the hot water and his labor might do something for me, *anything* to help.

"*...she was dead before it even came down the track.*"

I ached in the bath, physically biting my arm to keep from screaming. Eventually, I just laid my head on my arms, my legs braced as the water cooled and the bubbles of the bath disappeared around me. Soon, I was sitting in lukewarm water by myself.

I was unable to do anything else.

"Em?"

Royal had knocked first before speaking, but I hadn't said anything. Adjusting my legs, I cradled my arms. My sister had been murdered.

My sister had been assaulted.

The tears burned hot, and I closed my eyes, another knock on the door.

"Em, can I come in?"

I must have said yes only loud enough for him to hear. I did want him in here. I did want him with me. I was so alone in my head, and that scared me, *terrified* me, where I'd go if I let the thoughts in my head go rogue for too long. The door squeaked open, and a boy came in. I barely saw him, unable to even lift my head. It wasn't until Royal bent and sat on the floor beside the tub I even allowed myself to get a look of him.

I wasn't the only one who felt this, *experienced* this.

Normally lustrous green eyes were dull, bloodshot and lined with red. His sandy blond hair was all over the place, his fingers ran clear through many times. Pain laced his chiseled features, his strong jaw worked tight but even still, he didn't address any of it. He didn't acknowledge what he was feeling. Reaching into the bath, he took my sponge and brought it over my shoulders, the rough tips of his fingers brushing my skin.

I shivered, but not from the chill, leaning into each welcomed touch he gave me. I needed it. I needed his love so much right now.

Washing me seemed to be the only way for him to express it, at a loss for words himself as he bathed me. I sighed when he brought the water over my head, his fingers moving next to wash my hair. He took great care with this, lathering and rinsing before repeating, and after, he braided it. He'd done this before, and I knew he knew how.

He'd done this with her.

I stayed silent, screaming inside. The dull ache only eased a little by Royal's touch, one I wanted more and more of the more he touched me. His hand ran down my clean back, and I leaned into his touch, silently calling out for him to do more.

He obviously didn't hear me and reaching into the bathwater, he only did to get me up and to get me dry. I should have felt exposed before him, naked, and though I had, it wasn't physically. Mentally, I was showing him all my cards, all my pain.

I need you.

I still couldn't tell him what I needed, not when he dried me off with meticulous care, not when he spread my legs and touched me there. He did none of this sexually, only taking care of me until I was dry. He moved the thick towel over my breasts, and when he stood, desire laced his green eyes. Apparently, I'd misunderstood his disconnect, his want for me too.

Kiss me...

He wouldn't, and I knew he wouldn't, not now and with everything that happened. This was all too much, too fresh, and he wouldn't want to take from me.

But that didn't mean I couldn't take from him.

I pressed against him, forcing my mouth against his until he let me in. He dropped the towel, his fingers pinching my chin.

"Em..."

That was the first ounce of it, the first moment of pain he allowed me to feel. It emanated off him through his voice and in his touch when he braced my cheeks. I tugged at his shirt, and he worked it off, a perfect specimen of muscle and flesh before me.

"I fucking need you," he forced against my mouth. "I need out of all this, my head..."

For tonight. Though, he hadn't said it. It was what I needed too, some kind of release from all the voices and trauma in my mind. I wrapped my arms around his neck, and he lifted me from the tub, my naked flesh warm against his hard body.

He devoured me, not just my mouth but my soul. I bit at his lips with hungry pants, adrenaline burning within me as he took me out of the steaming bathroom with his strong arms.

We ended up in the bedroom, his big body easing on top of mine in his jeans. He was so hard, his fly straining at the seams. I unzipped him and eased both his pants and boxers down. He kicked out of them, then sat back on his haunches, taking the moments to stare at me before rejoining our mouths. I called out his name when he touched me between my legs, wanting him so deep.

"Em." He pulled my lips apart, ghosting soft kisses down to my chest. "My Em."

I closed my eyes, my nipples sensitive as he breathed heat

across them. He touched his teeth to them, tugging before taking a condom out of his jeans. He sheathed himself and when he entered me it felt so different this time than the others. The others hadn't been this, all this pain between us. The others hadn't been this exposed, no more secrets between us. He'd kept this all from me and with good reason.

A husky breath, and he threaded our fingers together, pressing them against the headboard as he rocked inside me. I cried out, telling him I loved him.

"I love you too," he admitted, his eyes and voice so sad. He pressed his face into the side of my neck, sighing. "I'm so sorry."

He might have been sorry for loving me, sorry for bringing me into all this. He might have been sorry for my pain, and I was sorry too. I was sorry we were in this together.

I was sorry that *this* felt like only the beginning.

His fingers drew softly across my shoulder later that night, my brain in and out of sleep. I wouldn't sleep long before waking up and eventually, just gave up on sleep entirely. I wrapped an arm around Royal's chest, and when he realized I was awake too, he kissed the top of my head. His fingers returned to my shoulder, and for long moments, I just listened to him breathe.

"It's because of Mira I even came out here," he said all of a sudden, a deep voice in a darkened room. He cradled my arm. "She's the reason we're both here and even know about all this."

I didn't understand, looking up at him. Even in the dark, he was majestic, a dream crafted into reality.

He played with my dark hair. "The night of everything... The night we found out about Paige, I got a text from her."

"A text when you were with me?" We'd been together that night, slept together like now.

He nodded. "It didn't come in until after I came over to see you. Woke up in the middle of the night when it pinged."

"What did it say?"

His expression shifted, going harder. "She said she had something for me. Found out something I'd want to know. I thought it was bullshit and put my phone down, but then I got another text. It said it was about Paige."

My attention alerted now, I sat up, resting on his chest.

He wet his lips. "Obviously, I went after that. She had me meet her at a twenty-four-hour diner. When I got there she had this file. She said it was Paige's case file. Claimed she swiped it from her dad the sheriff."

I supposed that was her dad, and since I knew that now, what he was saying made sense.

"She wanted to do a trade," he said, looking at me. "Said she'd give it to me if we could hook up. She's been after me since the second grade."

"What did you say?"

"The answer was a resounding no obviously, but I didn't tell her that. I needed that file, so I agreed just to get it. She was clearly fucking desperate for another hookup, and like an idiot, just gave up the file upon getting nothing but my word. I opened it with her, and needless to say, the whole thing was bullshit when I did."

"How so?"

"Well, for starters the whole thing was redacted to hell. Like permanent maker everywhere. Nothing could be seen but a few names and a couple details here and there, but that's not what bothered me the most. The case file was complete, *thick* like it'd been done well before that night."

That couldn't be possible. "How could the sheriff's office have a complete file on my sister's death if they'd just found out about her?"

"That's the thing. *They can't* and that's when I noticed the investigation wasn't even done by the Maywood Heights's sheriff's office. It was an outside contractor. A name I felt I'd heard before but I couldn't put my finger on where I'd heard it. Anyway, I called Mira on her bullshit, but I took that file because something weird was going on here. The sheriff's office knew about Paige's death before even the town did. For weeks judging by the case file. And remember that ring you found? That Court ring out at Route 80?"

Because I did, I swallowed. "Yes."

"Well, that was Paige's. *Mine* that I gave Paige before I got it replaced with the one I gave you. It was supposed to be hers after this whole thing. She must have lost it..."

I closed my eyes, chasing down the sickness.

"I looked into that after you gave it to me that day of the fire. Thinking I could find out something about where she'd gone."

He had missed a lot of school.

"But I came up with nothing." He squeezed my shoulder. "But now I know why. All this? There was nothing to find. She was *gone,* and the sheriff's office knew about that, but kept it quiet."

I shook. "But why would they? What does all this mean?"

He looked at me. "Well, at the time, it meant that I needed to look into things deeper. I left Mira that night at the diner and she threatened me. Said she knew about the haze and what 'us guys' were into. I guess she'd heard from some of the Court's other girlfriends. She thought holding that over my head would do something, get me to sleep with her, but I didn't give a shit. I had more important things to look into. The day of your sister's memorial service, I decided to drive up to the coroner's office. Figuring money talks, you know?"

I did know, and it had today.

He braced my arm. "Dr. Felton admitted he was told to destroy the file. He's only keeping it because of me, and I'm paying him like a goddamn employee for that. He was also even told to tamper with the physical evidence, any DNA on

Paige's physical remains tossed out, then wiped clean from the record before she was cremated."

I cringed. "Who told him to destroy the file in the first place? Do that?"

"The same company who did the investigation. Paige was taken out that night, killed before that train even came, and it was all covered up. And the whole story about the alcohol being in her system? The autopsy had nothing about that. The whole thing was bullshit, completely made up."

"But by who?" I asked, the reality of what all the guys tried to warn me about flooding back to me now. They'd been scared about something. Warned me about getting involved.

Royal's large chest rose with heavy breath and pulling me in, he kissed the top of my head again. "There's still a lot the guys and I have to piece together, but we do have our suspicions. There're some people involved in this, a few someones we think, and I get the feeling what *we know* is only the beginning."

CHAPTER
SEVEN

December

Things were starting to come together. Things were starting to make sense, and I squeezed a pillow that morning, my side cold. A divot in the bedding was all that remained of Royal Prinze the next morning. I assumed he was up and in the suite somewhere. I had slept a long time.

Easing into his spot, I wallowed there for longer than I liked, sought comfort there in ways I needed. Today, we needed to go over what was next, and *I* needed to be let in on whatever he and the guys were doing. They'd discovered something they obviously kept between themselves until now, and after last night, I knew why.

There was a murderer in the town of Maywood Heights.

The very thought shot a chill down my naked spine, and I closed my eyes, blocking out the sun. Whoever hurt my sister was still out there and maybe even still under our noses. There was a possibility, of course, they'd skipped town, but if someone got away with murder, as they clearly had, why would they? The person obviously had resources too in order to cover up such a thing. I closed my eyes in an attempt to block out the circumstances that surrounded the murder but to no avail. My sister had been out there by herself, her reality and now mine. My sister had been killed, raped.

Get out of this fucking bed.

I let go of the pillow, needing to be *her* strength now. I wouldn't let what happened to her go with her to the grave. I was still here, and as long as I was standing, whoever did this to her would get what was coming to them in the end. I'd get my revenge...

Even if I had to go to certain lengths.

I had no idea what those lengths might be, but I had a feeling Royal was already two steps ahead on it. Something had happened to him since I'd known him, a slow but steady transformation. He had a darkness inside him I saw more and more every day, and was something that was obviously heavily influenced by all this that happened with my sister. I had so many things I needed to know, questions dating back to that first time he pushed me away in California. Deciding it was time to get those answers, I got up, and when I found a shirt, it was Royal's. Shrugging it on, I went to the bathroom connected to the room. I got washed up real quickly, cleansing water on my face before brushing my teeth. After, I slid on a pair of bed pants from my bag to go with Royal's shirt. I went looking for him in the suite after I dressed, and as I smelled something cooking, *frying* as I made my way down the hallway, I smiled.

He cooks too.

He was so sweet, and in so many ways. His care was subtle but always present. Even when he was pushing me away, he was doing things for me, always there looking out for me. I realized now all the guys had in some way, shape, or form in the past, Jax, LJ, and Knight. I was highly surprised they didn't all come out for this trip just to be here. I guess I assumed Royal hadn't allowed that, on his own for this one.

"Royal?" I crept down the hallway, the suite incredibly warm and smelled so stinkin' good. It was a smell I couldn't identify, something hot but nothing like bacon or eggs. I appreciated those smells despite being vegan. I didn't have to eat the food to know it still smelled good, and I wasn't ignorant to good-smelling things.

What's he making?

"Royal?" I found him in the kitchen, well... at least someone. Whoever was whistling a happy tune, shaking his chiseled hips in his designer jeans. He was a little shorter than Royal and the buzzed haircut definitely told me it wasn't him. I caught looks of the guy in the kitchen over the bar and must have announced myself because Jax turned around with a frying pan in his hand.

He grinned. "Ah, *mon cherie! Comment allez vous?*"

My eyebrows had to have jumped at least the height of my forehead. He spoke French? I shook my head, only to see LJ skirt through the kitchen with a spoon. The tall blond scooped some of whatever Jax had in the pan right out of it, blowing on a sample before tasting it.

Jax frowned. "What the fuck, dude?"

LJ whacked him with the wooden spoon before tossing it into the kitchen sink and washing his hands behind the bar. He flashed white teeth at me. "You'll have to forgive him. He took all of a semester of French before switching over to German."

Looking hurt, Jax placed the spatula to his chest. "What can I say? My family has ties to the motherland."

"More like to Hitler." LJ dodged quick when Jax attempted to swing the frying pan full of food at him, and chuckling, LJ came out of the kitchen. Finding me, the extremely tall blond boy with a rather long wingspan threw an arm around me, bringing me into a hug. "Hey, good to see you."

It was surprisingly good to see him too, and Jax. I was actually just thinking about all of them.

I hugged him back. "You too. Where's Royal? Knight?"

"Went for some OJ and some smacks." LJ came away. He pointed over the bar. "This one's cooking you both out of house and home."

Appearing hurt again, Jax came out of the kitchen with his frying pan and spatula. "Am not. I'm just trying out a new recipe my moms taught me."

Folding his arms, LJ lounged back against the suite's dining room table. He tossed a nod at me. "Jax's moms are celebrity chefs."

"Only during the week." Jax ventured over to the dining table too, which I now realized had quite the spread. There was a bowl of cut melon in the center, oatmeal and various things used to sweeten and flavor it next to that, and carafe of what looked like milk.

"You're vegan, right?" Jax asked, his frying pan filled with what looked like eggs but didn't smell like it. From the looks of it, there were peppers, mushrooms, and some kind of meat mixed in there with yellow crumbles. He raised the pan. "I present a vegan tofu scramble. I've been dying to make this. One of my moms is vegan too."

"How did you know I was vegan and where did you even get all this stuff?" I asked, laughing when I took one of the seats.

Jax pushed the food onto my plate, and it looked hella good. "Royal. He had all the food already in the fridge."

Of course he did, another one of those things he did. He could fool the world all he wanted with his brooding attitude.

He was still sweet as hell.

Kind of in awe, I shook my head. "What did you use for meat?"

"Seitan." Jax placed the pan in the center on an oven mitt, and when LJ frowned—he'd taken a seat next to me and *hadn't* gotten served—Jax threw a hand at him. "Um, all this so isn't for you, bro," he chided before wiggling his eyebrows at me. "What do you think, December?"

He appeared very excited for my response so I sampled what he made.

"Dude," I basically moaned. Grabbing another forkful, I shoved it into my mouth. "What the fuck?"

"I know, right?" His grin strong, Jax backed away, heading toward the kitchen. "Wait until you have it with chocolate almond milk. We only put regular on the table."

"You know, you really don't have to open and consume everything in the fridge? We're checking out later today."

Royal appeared from behind my chair when I turned, never failing to look hot as hell. He had his North Face jacket on, his cheeks flushed and red. I started to get up, but he came to me, a bag of groceries in his hands. He kissed my cheek. "Good morning, princess."

I'd never *not* like him calling me that, calling me anything really. I just loved him saying my name. I loved loving him.

"Hey." I pulled back. "You got groceries?"

"Got three more mouths to feed." He wagged blond eyebrows. "Four if you count Knight's gladiator ass."

"Shut the fuck up." Knight came around the corner in his big-ass puffer coat, and I was reminded by how he'd let me wear that once. He'd saved me, literally giving me the coat off his back. He came into the room with about three more bags to each one Royal had. Knight placed them on the bar. "I paid for all this shit so I eat what I want."

The guys chuckled, Royal too when he stripped off his jacket. He put it on the back of my chair and started to take the groceries to the kitchen, but Knight told him he had it covered. He must have not been too mad at what Royal said because he not only put all the groceries away but set out place settings for the other guys. After he was done, he hung his coat and took off a gray hat from dark locks.

"I see you started without me." Royal threw an arm around my front, smelling of heat and boy. He pressed his face into my cheek. "Sorry I wasn't here when you woke up."

"So is this how it's going to be now?" Jax directed a fork at Royal. He'd taken his seat and started eating too. He grinned. "You being all 'Kept' and bitch ass?"

"December's not Kept." LJ pulled the words right out of Royal's mouth and so quick Royal hadn't even had to say them. LJ winked. "Clearly, look at her neck. You know she's wearing his ring."

"Yeah." Royal hugged both arms around me. "She's in. Obviously, since we took this trip."

"So she knows everything?" Despite bringing in so much food, Knight didn't eat any of it when he sat down. He folded his fingers. "She knows about everything?"

The tone of the room changed with the very words, and even though Knight had said them, his expression fell as well. Dark eyebrows narrowed, his eyes looking away, and nothing but the clanks and clamor of Jax's eating filled the silence. Eventually, Jax stopped doing that too, just staring at Royal and me.

Royal pushed hands down my arms. "I told her why she and I are here and what brought me here initially."

"So she doesn't know who we think had something to do with it?" Knight was very blunt, but I could hold my own with him. I could hold my own with all of them.

I sat back. "He told me he had some suspicions but hasn't said whom."

All eyes shifted to Royal in that moment, and at that point, he took the empty chair next to mine. He spun it around, sitting on the back right next to me. "Remember when I said there was a private company that did your sister's investigation? A company I thought I recognized?"

I nodded, and he placed a hand on mine, threading them together.

"Well, I later did after I found out what happened to Paige. I Googled and realized it's one of my dad's companies, Bankable Assets & Holdings LLC."

The room spun, and I thought I'd throw up what little I'd eaten. The tofu turned into a mass in my gut, the bile charging up my throat like molten lava.

"Are you saying your dad..." I couldn't even get the words out, swallowing hard. "Are you saying your dad *did* *this* to my sister? He touched my sister..."

"No, December. No." He brought my hands in with his. "Fortunately for him, my fucker of a dad has an alibi."

"He was with us." LJ raised a hand off the table. "We were all called away to help with some Court business."

"The Court has a gala every year." Royal panned in my direction, frowning. "Senior members make a big deal about it. I'd been avoiding it, honestly. Dad nailed me that night."

"Roped my grandfather in to help him do it," Knight grunted. "They all make a big deal out of that shit, so we went."

"We shouldn't have gone." The words were said by Jax. Done with his food too, he threaded his fingers. "She was alone."

"She insisted on it." Royal's attention shifted to me. "Hazes are supposed to be done singularly, and even if they weren't, Paige would have made us leave. She had to push me to leave in the end."

In the end... the story came out again. He was there that night, they *all* were like I'd been told before.

"So he just covered it up?" I asked. "Why?"

Royal dampened his lips. "That's one of the things we have no clue about. I assumed it was to protect me. I bet a lot of it had to do with me."

He had done a haze that night, he and the other boys...
How fucked up.

I lowered my head, and my shoulders were rubbed, Royal on one side and LJ on the other.

"That's not all, though, Royal." Knight leaned forward. "Tell her everything."

"Everything?" I looked over and Royal's jaw moved.

He sighed. "There's a lot to this, December. A whole fucking lot, and we're still working it all out."

"Enlighten me." I needed to be goddamn enlightened. I needed the truth. "I told you I want to know everything."

"You don't know what you're asking, December." LJ grappled our attention, his mouth in a hard frown. "There's a lot of pieces to this. It's all dangerous."

"Well, you're in it," I stated, and they confirmed with nods. My throat jumped. "Tell me everything. I'm going to be in it too."

The room was silent again with no one eating. Royal eased his chair closer. "The minute I found out about Paige I wanted revenge. I wanted to find out whoever it was and *end them.* With my bare hands if I had to."

I took his, squeezing them, and he did back.

He touched his forehead to mine. "I had this whole plan, Em. Even roped in Mira. I got close to her. That's why I came with her to Paige's reception. I needed her close. My only link to the sheriff's office and finding out the truth."

I looked up, and he placed a hand to my cheek.

His thumb brushed my skin. "But then you wanted to leave. Fuck, did I want to leave with you."

"He did."

I left his hand, LJ cringing when I faced him. LJ frowned. "We begged him not to, December."

"We had to find out who did this to Paige." Knight shrugged. "No other option."

"But we are sorry, all of us and especially me." LJ touched my shoulder. "I lied to you."

"You all did for me." Royal gazed around. "You did for me. You knew what we needed to do, what *I* needed to do."

"We did it for Paige," Jax said. "It wasn't all his fault, December. Letting you go? It was all of us. We wanted to protect you."

And I was starting to understand that now. There wasn't much out there that would make me lie or hurt Royal or now, any of them. But my sister was one of those exceptions. I'd do anything.

"So that day we were supposed to leave," I stated, focusing on Royal. "The guys convinced you not to go with me?"

"Surprisingly, my father was the one to make me change my mind in the end." He frowned. "He threatened me. He threatened *you* to the point where... I honestly questioned how much him covering this whole thing up had to do with me."

CHAPTER
EIGHT

Royal

This was hard, admitting all this to her, but it was the fucking truth and she deserved it. I called the guys all here today for support. We were all involved in this, and we all had to be here.

I took December's hand again, so warm. I was putting her through the fucking wringer, this beautiful and sweet girl. I kissed her hand. "He told me to stay away from you. Threatened me if I didn't."

I took such a beating that night, one none of them, not even Jax, LJ, and Knight knew about. I kept that one close to the cuff.

December touched my cheek, her dark hair skating across her lovely skin. I wanted to touch her too and I did, my thumb parting her lips.

"So you pushed me away," she concluded. She nodded. "You put me on a bus."

I put her as far away from this place and my fucking dad as I could. He had basically unlimited resources, could hurt her and her family. I couldn't take the risk, not at that point. I nodded. "I did."

"And the whole thing with Mira?" she stated, looking hurt. I hate that I fucking hurt her. It killed me. Still even today. She swallowed. "Being with her when I came back?"

The same. Once I knew she was back and in my life, I had to put up a brick wall.

I folded my fingers behind her neck. "I was going to do whatever I had to, to keep you away. To keep you safe." And I had ultimately, some of the things still sickening me. I had to touch someone else to put up a divider from her. "I let her think it was because of the blackmail. She knew about the haze that night, how her dad helped cover it up. I let her think that's what our relationship was. Easy."

A shuddered breath shook her shoulders. "But why? Why would your dad even threaten me in the first place?"

"It definitely put my back up. All of our backs." I gazed around the room at the guys, getting their nods. "We didn't know if it was just about me at this point. If who attacked Paige was a drifter…"

"Or someone in house." Knight whispered the words, working his hands like he was going to annihilate a mother-fucker. I knew he would. We all would to get to the truth. "This brotherhood is tight."

"So tight." Jax wet his lips. "It could be anybody in the Court, so we made the decision to move into Windsor House."

"I told my dad the move was because I wanted to get more involved with Court." I smirked. "He leaped for fucking joy."

"My grandpa too." Knight lifted a brawny shoulder. He laced his fingers across his chest. "We've never been into the Court like they all have."

"It was a good cover." I frowned, my eyebrows narrowing hard. "Gave us time."

"For?"

Beautiful, nut-brown eyes stared back at me, and I touched December's cheek. "Remember those texts your sister sent me? The ones that said she was leaving and getting out of town?"

Those haunted me for such a long time, the presence of them causing me to deny our ultimate reality. It wasn't until I'd seen the proof of Paige's death, the images of what some sick fuck did to her body and what the autopsy report said that I allowed myself to actually believe something more to the story was going on. I finally admitted my friend hadn't just skipped town and gotten in an accident, but was murdered and someone was covering it up.

"Yeah." December squeezed my hand. "You said she sent them the next day. How was that possible?"

"It's not," I basically growled, knowing how false they were. "We had that redacted case folder *un*-redacted."

"Cost basically all our college tuition to do it." We all looked at Jax who shrugged. "What? It did."

"What did it say?" December leaned in, and I took her other hand.

I called for strength. "You sister didn't get hit a town over. She died, right there at Route 80 on the tracks, and a train later came through and dragged her away. She was ultimately found in Corrington Meadows but the murder happened there first. Those text were false. Someone sent them to me so I wouldn't come looking, *knew* to send them to me of all people. That's another reason why I thought my dad trying to protect me wasn't just for me. Someone knew that I knew Paige. We looked everywhere for that cell phone. Tore up Windsor House, our houses."

The color bled from December's face. "She probably knew them, didn't she? The person who hurt her?"

"Most likely, yeah."

December's skin paled a few more shades, and I wanted

to stop. I didn't want to do this to her anymore, but she wanted the truth. She wanted to be a part of this.

My throat jumped, so many things about this fucked up. "We've had everyone followed. Our dads, uncles, grand-fathers."

"Everybody but one."

We all panned to Knight, but he had eyes on me.

Knight crossed a leg at the knee. "We haven't looked into who actually started all this, the reason why your sister even did that haze and was out there in the first place."

"You mean her girlfriend?" December sat up, and I bobbed my head once. "But why?"

"We honestly hadn't even thought to." LJ rested lanky arms on the table. "Not until Royal went down to California to see Paige and thought of her ex."

"That had been my mistake," I said. "Since Paige was clearly assaulted, I only kept my radar on the men of this town, but a woman could have been involved. It was real bad blood between your sister and her, Em, and I feel like a fucking idiot for not thinking about her. The reason they broke up? Really broke up was because the woman was married and wouldn't leave her husband."

Her lips parted. "What?"

"Yeah, it's true. Paige knew she was married. Knew it was wrong. Even still, she continued to see her. The woman led her to believe she was end game, toyed with her for months."

December cringed. "What happened?"

"She wasn't end game." I looked up. "I don't know whether the woman chickened out or if it all was a lie… the whole thing concluded when her husband caught the two of them together. *In the woman's house*, her bed. Paige was naked, embarrassed, but her ex let that fucker she called a husband toss Paige out without any clothes into the street like she was trash."

The horror I still remembered in Paige's eyes that day after it happened, and it took so much coaxing to even get the truth out of her. She was so embarrassed, heartbroken. Both parties had no business doing what they'd been doing, but it'd only been one to be tossed out naked into the road while the other slammed the door in the other's face.

Paige had been enraged, wanting ultimate revenge. She could have gotten it from us, but she wanted it for herself. She wanted to be moving the pieces of the Court behind the scenes, to end this woman's life like she knew the pull of the Court could. The Court could destroy lives, the benefits of living in a small town run by few. A few power plays, and the woman would be stripped of everything she held dear, to feel just an ounce of what she allowed Paige to feel. Thinking back, maybe that's why everything had turned out the way it had. Revenge was a delicate and dark line to tread.

I wished it had been me in the end, that she let me do this for her. My friend might actually be alive, my soul able to be traded if only to keep hers.

December was shaking at this point, and I brought her into me. Her face had transferred two shades of pink, the flush close to accompanying tears but she held them inside.

Her lashes lowered. "Who is she, Royal?" she asked, easing closer to me. "Who is this woman who destroyed Paige's life?"

I didn't have an answer for her but couldn't admit that and stayed silent. It was Knight who ultimately talked, my voice for me when I didn't have one. How ironic since he was as quiet as he was.

"He doesn't know," he'd said. He frowned. "None of us do."

This clearly shocking December, she sat up.

I cupped her arm. "She didn't tell us, tell me. I think she thought we'd do something if we knew."

"Damn right we would." LJ smiled, and I did a little too. We'd do anything for her, anything.

I wet my lips. "She was supposed to tell me, all of us, after she finished the haze. She promised."

"So her secret dies with her." Fury ghosted December's delicate features, dark hair against her flush cheeks. "And this woman gets away with everything she might have done in connection to the murder? Actually, she had everything to do with this. She's the reason Paige even got into this stupid shit."

What she said was all true, reality. A harsh breath flew from my lips. "We hoped finding her cell phone would lead us to the right place. Whoever has it. Hurt her, a direct link."

"Or doesn't." She threw fingers through her hair. "What if they destroyed it? You really think someone would be that stupid to hold on to something like that?"

"You'd be surprised," I said. "All it takes is one slipup for this whole thing to fall apart. Especially, if there are a lot of moving pieces."

With my dad involved, there would be. He covered his tracks, but since he clearly didn't do this, the other party or parties were rogue variables. They could slip up where he wouldn't, and that, and only that, gave us hope.

"But we've checked everywhere for that thing, Royal," Jax said, usually the voice of hope. He never gave up, always happy to fight another day. This whole thing had messed us all up. He laced his fingers. "We literally have torn up this entire town for that phone, and we haven't found it. December might be right."

The other guys said nothing and maybe that's what they were thinking too, but I couldn't go there. Not yet. I needed hope. I *needed* to bring justice for my friend. If I didn't, I had nothing, couldn't stomach to walk free in this world when my friend was dead, and the person responsible was still out there. It'd destroy me.

Soft hands moved over mine, and when I gazed up, December was facing the room.

"This might be out there and I don't know where all you guys have already searched, but," she started, then found my eyes, "have you checked your father's vault? You know, the one at the jewelry store?"

Blinking, my eyes narrowed. "Dad's vault? How do you know about that?"

I admit we hadn't checked it, his customers' valuables in there, and though he had his own, he kept the real good stuff overseas in international bank vaults all over the world. We'd have checked those, but doing so was basically impossible without his authorization.

December chewed her lip a little. "Ramses had my Kept necklace there," she said, making my stomach sour. "Back when we told everyone we were dating, I went down there and got it. Your dad was there that day and took me into the vault to get it. Ramses couldn't do it. He'd just been to the woods that night."

Because we'd hazed him, all of this fucking darkness. I just wanted to be rid of it. I gripped her hands, and LJ touched my shoulder.

"We haven't checked your dad's vault, Royal," he said. "Hadn't thought to."

"She knows about all this two seconds, and she's already helping." A smile from Knight, a rare occurrence indeed. He tipped a chin at Jax. "Your cousin Benjamin still work at the jewelry store?"

December grimaced for some reason. "That guy's your cousin? He was such a douche that day at the store."

"Uh, second cousin." Jax raised his hands. "And yeah, why?"

"See if you can get his keys," I said, Knight and I of the same mind. "They'd be easier to get than my dad's."

It wouldn't be impossible but definitely easier if he plucked them off his cousin. My father would notice right away, and we didn't want to risk him finding out.

"But how can we get in there after that?" December shifted her gaze between us. "Your dad had to take me down. He said only he had access to the vault and the box itself took his fingerprint to open."

"The boxes take four prints actually," I said. "And only the same have access to the vault."

December's lips parted, and I brushed hair out of her face.

"Only a Prinze can get down there," I said to her. "My mom. My sister, my dad, and me."

CHAPTER
NINE

December

The ride back to Maywood Heights was a quick one. If anything, it was only made a smidgen longer by Jax, who not only chose to ride back to town and school with us but made Royal's life a living hell by singing to every song that graced the radio. Frankly, I found the whole thing hilarious, a glimmer of joy in the fucked-up-ness that was about to go down the moment we returned home. We planned to visit the jewelry store sometime after school, and that's when this whole thing would begin again.

Royal took the ride home in good stride, his arm around me while he drove, and I think the only reason he did put up with Jax was because he found that glimmer too. He wanted that lightness, the opposite of the dark that was about to take us all away again. Since we checked out so early, we'd been able to get on the road and ultimately, home before school began. I checked in with Dad right as we pulled up into the Windsor Preparatory parking lot. The academy was filled to the brim with students and poshness, all in their school uniforms. We were in ours too, something we'd packed, and the boys had changed as well before leaving the hotel.

"You made it in okay?" Dad actually checked in with *me*, hella serious I guess with his forty-eight-hour deadline. He'd wanted to make sure I arrived at school the way I said I would, and since I had, I attempted to chill him the fuck out. "December, did you hear me?"

Apparently, my attempt at chill was friggin' shitty, and I lifted a hand to Royal to wait. He'd started to head toward the old, brick building filling up with students. Knight and LJ had tailed us the entire time back into the city, flanking my boyfriend, but they all stopped when Royal halted them. Royal tilted his head. "Everything okay?"

I covered my phone. "Yeah, just Dad freaking out," I said, waving the group on. "It'll take a second."

But me waving them on wasn't happening, the force of boys standing their ground. In the end, they came back, and I guess I wasn't surprised. Too much had simply happened for them to leave me alone. They all stood there while my dad let in on me, but eventually, Royal dismissed his men in waiting when it really started to be a long time. He gave the boys fist pounds before slinging an arm around my waist and waiting. His scent immediately surrounded me as he rested his chin on my shoulder, possessive. I had a feeling that's just how things were about to be.

I sighed into the phone, my dad doing his own possessive thing for some weird reason. "I'm fine, Dad. I made it home. I'm about to head into school."

A few more moments and Royal lifted his watch, tapping at the time. We really didn't have a lot of it before the class warning bells hit, and I understood that.

"I gotta get to class," I urged into the line. "I'm right outside."

"I understand that, but I'm not done yet. In fact, put me on FaceTime."

Thrown, I blanched. "What?"

"I said put me on FaceTime, December, and I'm not joking."

So obviously not, I did what I was told, and Royal stood back. Instantly, my dad's face was on the phone screen, in some kind of office. I assumed his, a large window in the background. He also wore a suit and looked pissed the fuck off...

At least until he saw my face. Something visually settled there, and I didn't understand. My lips parted. "Dad..."

"Show me the school."

I did, angling the phone so he could see the flooded parking lot and later, the academy behind me. Seeing that, his broad shoulders relaxed too but stiffened a bit when Royal appeared into view. I knew this since I could see Royal as well on the screen with me in the background. He hadn't gone far, just given me space for the call, but the moment he came into view on the screen, my dad's expression changed again. Pissed the fuck off took on a new meaning, and I shifted to put Royal out of focus. I guess Dad wasn't too keen on his baby girl running off into the night and taking time off school with her new boyfriend. I got that, but he was hella on right now.

Dad threw fingers through his hair and everything, dark like mine but obviously not as long. "Good," he huffed. "Well, get off to it and call me when you get home."

"Why?"

"Just do it, December," he gritted. Pausing, he took a look around his office before focusing his attention back on me. "These are strange times, don't you think? You should know. We lost your sister, didn't we?"

That's what he was worried about? Losing me? He hadn't been concerned before.

"Okay," I said. These definitely were strange times. I

supposed Mira's death put him over the edge, but she'd killed herself. "I will."

"You will?"

"I will. I promise."

"Okay." This seemed to calm him down. He lowered the phone to stand on his desk, taking a seat. "Have a good day, then."

"You too."

He clicked me off, and after sliding the phone into my bag, I turned to find Royal. His arm fell around my shoulders again, and he took my book bag from me, slinging it on his shoulder with his.

"Any idea what that was about?" he asked during our strides, but since I didn't, I could only shrug. I guess these strange times had finally made it into my house too, with my dad. Who would have thought?

Though the morning started off weird, at least first and second period settled back into some type of normalcy. The whispers had definitely been there, though, despite a little time past. Mira killing herself had justifiably set a tone, and Royal, Jax, LJ, Knight, and I weren't spared from it. People talked. People gossiped about her, and I got to hear the whispers of it at the beginning and in between classes. The only place I was spared from it was *in* class and that's because the teachers were lecturing and wouldn't have the chatter. Any veer off of focus was quickly steered in the direction of numbers or text and continued that way until the end of second period for me that morning. Mr. Pool got a knock on his door, and he paused, beckoning in the person with a couple words. Something told me the English lit instructor didn't expect our headmaster, Principal Hastings, to show up...

Nor the two members of campus security who accompanied him.

The presence of them stopped class entirely, Principal

Hastings leading the train. He walked right up to Mr. Pool, waving to speak to him semi-privately. Well, it was as private as it could get with the two being in front of an entire classroom of senior students. I exchanged a quick glance with Birdie before gazing back at Royal, Jax, LJ, Knight and the rest of their Court crew. We had assigned seats, which was the only reason I wasn't back there with them.

Royal's cool green gaze grappled on to me too, his expression grim.

Especially when he was called to stand.

"Mr. Prinze?" Principal Hastings called again. He waved him this time. "Could you come with me, please?"

The trivial "oohs" of a class full of juvenile-minded individuals trickled through the room, but Royal played it off with a smirk, even smacking LJ's hand before getting up and coming forward. LJ received the hit in good stride, but his bro's expression was definitely tense when he let go, all the guys were. They stared at Royal in unity as their friend made his way to the front and eventually, out of the room with the security staff. They'd guided them to come with them and after a nod to Mr. Pool, Principal Hastings followed them.

What the fuck?

I shot a look toward the back of the room. Jax and LJ shrugged, but Knight's sneer could have frightened a toddler. I raised a hand. "Mr. Pool, can I have the hall pass? You know, Aunt Flo?"

This got some snickers, and Birdie covered her mouth. A small "what the fuck?" left her lips, and as I watched the color drain from Mr. Pool's face at clearly ladies' troubles, I knew what I said got the job done. He reached into his desk, pulling out the pass.

Instantly, I got up, and when he handed it to me, he leaned in.

"A simple, 'I need the hall pass' will do for the future, December," he said, a clear to his throat before letting me go with it. It astounded me that in this turn of the century a cis male such as himself could clearly still be bothered by a little period blood.

I shook my head a little when I got into the hallway and, after gazing around, stood there a second to figure out my next move. I had no idea where Royal would have been skirted off to, but I started in the direction of the headmaster's office. If they wanted to talk to him, they'd do so in private most likely. I had to pass the north hall on the way, and I was glad I took that route because that's exactly where I ended up finding Royal and the people who took him.

They were searching his locker.

"Can I ask what the hell you guys are looking for?" Hands in his pockets, Royal allowed them to do the search, not that he had much choice with the headmaster on standby.

Principal Hastings's lips curled. "That's a warning, Mr. Prinze. Don't use that language in my halls."

"What's this about, then?" Royal lifted and dropped his hands, and from the distance, I caught a glance of who flanked his other side.

The sheriff, the legit sheriff of Maywood Heights, stood there, hands on his hips and in full uniform. What was even weirder about that was the school's security staff stood *behind him*. That's when I realized Maywood Heights *cops* searched Royal's locker. Real cops like he was a criminal.

"You'll let the men do their job, son," Principal Hastings said, and Royal grimaced.

"I'm not your *son*, Headmaster," Royal returned, his eyes dark. He forced his arms over his chest. "And I think I have a right to know why my personal property is being searched."

Principal Hastings honed in. "These lockers are *my* property, Mr. Prinze."

"And *we* have a search warrant." Sheriff Ashford pinned the document with a motion against Royal's chest. The man looked a far cry different than he had last time I'd seen him.

He appeared less like a grieving father and more a pissed-off sheriff. I didn't understand and headed down the hallway.

Royal instantly noticed, his arms lowering to his sides. "December?"

The whole party turned in the hallway, and when Royal started to leave the line, the sheriff got him by the arm. "We're not done here."

Royal wrestled away but Principal Hastings stopped him, getting between the both of us. He put his hands up, his sneer in my direction. "Why are you here, Ms. Lindquist?"

"Bathroom." I held up the pass. "What's going on?"

Distracted, Principal Hastings gave room for Royal to get a hand around and on me. He pulled me over. "These creeps are searching my locker. I don't know why—"

"Well, you will now," one of the cops said, shifting everyone's attention that way. Wearing blue gloves, the officer had a cell phone between two fingers, a cell phone that wasn't Royal's. I didn't recognize it, but I knew it wasn't my boyfriend's. I'd seen it a lot the past couple days since we'd been staying together.

Sheriff Ashford's eyes were wild as he took it. He snatched the phone with force, slamming it up against Royal's chest so hard he let go of me. The sheriff bared his teeth. "What the *hell* is this, boy?"

Royal shook his head, his eyes flashing wide. "I have no idea, sir. It's not mine…"

"I know it's not." Sheriff Ashford pushed him again, pushed him so hard. "It's my damn daughter's. Get this little shit in handcuffs."

"What—"

Without a thought, the men did, grabbing and throwing Royal into a set of lockers. His face hit so hard his eyes shut.

"Royal!"

A hand came out, pulling me back. "Back off, Ms.

Lindquist," Principal Hastings said, his hand grappled tight on my arm. "Let the men do their job."

"I didn't fucking do anything!" Royal roared, the cops strong-arming him. At this point, Sheriff Ashford had given the phone to one of the officers and was cuffing Royal himself, using more force than he should have on a teenage boy.

He forced Royal's face into the lockers. "You have the right to remain silent," he started, basically spitting at Royal as he went into the Miranda rights. He quickly finished his spiel and pressed Royal's face to the metal again. "And you did fucking do something. Otherwise, your name wouldn't be all over my daughter's suicide letter we found this morning."

"What!" Pulled off the locker, Royal thrust a shoulder, bucking. "That's bullshit."

"Is it? I guess we'll find out." Sheriff Ashford threw Royal at the other cops. "Get him in the car."

The men took Royal, but when I started to go again, Principal Hastings's hand dug into my arm to the point where it pinched. I was jerked back, almost falling, and the only thing Royal seemed to be aware of then was me.

"Fucking let her go!" he growled, fighting the men hard, but he was in no state to help me when two armed officers were all over him. They tugged him away, Royal bucking the entire time, and I couldn't go either since Principal Hastings had me. The headmaster got me to my feet but he wasn't letting me go.

Sheriff Ashford raised his hat, his face beet red. "Your cooperation is appreciated."

"Of course. Our halls are always open to the Maywood Heights Sheriff's Office," Principal Hastings said, holding me by both arms now. He had to...

I was screaming my fucking head off.

"Royal!"

"December!" Royal hollered, roaring again. "Let me go!"

They didn't, didn't let either one of us go, and the bell rang, letting class out. The halls immediately filled, and it was only after they clustered to the point of suffocation Principal Hastings released me.

"I hope you're going to class, Ms. Lindquist," he said from behind me, the asshole. I didn't look back. I just ran after Royal. I could hear him screaming, calling out my name over the blaring noise in the hall, and I only saw him a little because students were making way for the arrest. He was being carted away in front of *everyone*, embarrassed in front of everyone, and Principal Hastings let that happen.

"Royal!"

"December?" Knight grabbed me, LJ and Jax right behind him. Knight's lips parted. "What's going on?"

"Royal's being arrested. We have to stop them!"

The boys could see now, see it all, and immediately started parting the crowd. They did for me to run and them to follow, the process made easy with Knight. He bowled over mother-fuckers, no one a match for his size and speed.

"Get the fuck out of the way!" he charged, but not quick enough. By the time we got outside, they already had Royal down the steps of the school and into a squad car. A line of school security stood between us and the car, so we could only watch on, letting them arrest Royal.

The police shut the door in Royal's face behind the security line, and by then, the entire student body stood on the school's brick insignia to witness. The squad car's lights flashed, and next thing we all knew, they were driving away, Royal inside.

Royal faced the back window, watching me. He wasn't even concerned about himself, all focus on me.

"Get back to class, everyone." Principal Hastings pushed his way through the crowd. "I won't hesitate to take away your prom. Be the example for Mr. Prinze."

I made eye contact with him then, tears in my eyes, and he

did nothing but fold his arms. He stared right at me, his look so fucking smug. He clearly believed he'd done a good job here today, and it took all I had not to punch him in his face for what he'd allowed to happen so publicly...

The bruises he'd no doubt left on my arm would only support the violence.

CHAPTER
TEN

December

The crew and I were in for a long day ahead of us. Knight, Jax, LJ, and I had to wait until school let out for us to do anything, and after, the boys were immediately heading to their cars and making calls. Their focus to get information on what was going on and Royal's place in it started the moment we left the school campus, but since I wasn't focused on making any calls and just getting to Royal, I did that. The boys gave me the combination to Royal's locker, so I got his keys. Before I knew it, I was in his Audi and speeding off before even the boys could catch up with me. Jax actually yelled at me, wanting to come with, and I would have let him if I fucking cared enough to slow down.

Knowing he could get a ride from the other guys, I sped on, blowing through traffic lights and even stop signs. It was reckless, yes. It was stupid even more so, but I didn't care. Royal was arrested for having some connection with Mira, and that was bullshit. He'd told me he had no idea why she'd killed herself, and I believed him. We weren't

doing this crap to each other anymore, keeping secrets. I
believed him, so I knew whatever was going on now was full
of shit.

It had to be.

I took up about three parking spaces when I parked. For
one, because I didn't know how to frickin' drive this thing,
and for second, because Royal was actually coming out of
county lockup the moment I showed up. He was basically
being dragged down the steps by his father who not only
looked pissed the hell off but showed him that when he
jerked him. I didn't know whether Royal was over that or just
standing up for himself because the next thing I knew Royal
shoved his father back. Like literally shoved him to the point
where he stumbled in his leather shoes and trench coat. The
swing came out of nowhere, and it had to have because it
caught Royal right in his eye. His dad sent him down for the
count, and I threw myself out of the car.

"Royal!"

This gained Mr. Prinze's attention in ways it had before,
the man assaulting his son only for other witnesses to see. I'd
been that witness two times now.

"This is family business," the man in a trench coat
growled at me, and with what I knew now about him, it took
all I had in me not to attack him. He covered up my sister's
murder, but right now, he definitely didn't need to know I
knew that. It was pertinent so we could keep up our search
for evidence. Because of that fact and only that, I ended up on
my knees in the chilly winds instead of punching the man's
lights out.

"Royal…" His eyebrow was bleeding, not a direct hit this
time to his eye. He lifted a hand as if he was fine, and seeing
that, Mr. Prinze charged forward.

He grabbed Royal's arm. "I said this is family business—"

"Fuck off, Dad." Royal got to his feet, pulling away from
his dad and grabbing me. He did so to shield me, but when

his dad appeared to be coming at him again, *I* did the shielding.

I put a hand out, one between the both of them.

"He's coming home with me," I gritted, daring that man to come at me and strike my boyfriend again. I shook my head. "Sorry, Mr. Prinze, but he is."

Truth was, I wasn't sorry. I wanted him to fucking *bleed*, but I needed Royal safe. I didn't know what he'd do to him if they went home together.

I think what I said surprised both of them, Royal's eyebrows jumping just as steadfast as his father's. It must not have frazzled him long because in the end, Royal chose me.

"Leave, Dad," he said, standing up to him again. His throat jumped. "I appreciate you bailing me out, but I'm not going with you. Sorry."

He seemed even less sorry than I did, and eyes wild, I wondered if Mr. Prinze would strike us both, strike me. A glance at his watch took him in another direction.

Eyes of a dull green shifted our way. They weren't bright like his son's. They were dark, cold. Mr. Prinze's eyes narrowed. "You're lucky I'm late for a flight out of town on business. You haven't heard the end of this, boy. You have to come home eventually."

He may be right, but he wasn't going home now. Not tonight and definitely nowhere with him.

Done with us, Mr. Prinze shifted on his patent leather shoes, and like clockwork, a chauffeured car pulled up right in from of him.

I pushed arms around Royal's waist, and Royal brought me in as his dad got inside. He rubbed my arm, turning away from his dad, who gave us both a death stare. The man quickly peeled off, and after, Royal kissed the top of my head.

"You're braver than me," he said, and I laughed, but only for a short while. The blood on his eyebrow dripped a stream down his cheek. I attempted to touch it, but Royal squinted.

He angled his cheek away. "Don't freak. I'm sure it looks worse than it is."

"Maybe, but either way, you're coming with me," I said, taking his hand. "We're going home."

———

I'd been so quick to the precinct I missed Jax, LJ, and Knight in the end. They arrived after us, and Royal and I got the text while we were on my dad's couch. He wasn't home from work yet, just the two of us, and currently, I was on my knees in front of Royal, cleaning up his face. I dabbed at the cut above his eye with some stuff that made him curse, not the best at this, but I think I got the right thing. The liquid bubbled over his wound, and he had stopped bleeding.

"The guys want to know where we are," Royal said, reading his phone. Touching the cut with a cotton ball, I got him good in the eyebrow again and he lowered his phone with a cringe. "You trying to heal me or hurt me, princess?"

"Shut up." I put some ointment on it, then handed him a princess Band-Aid for being smart. "Put it on yourself since I can't do this right."

I started to get up, but he got me by the hips. A quick maneuver and I was on his lap, straddling his hips.

He settled my weight on him, slinging heavy arms around my waist.

"I want you to do it," he said, giving me big, green puppy dog eyes. "Please."

It'd be hard to deny him with as warm and as hot as he was, and in the end, I succumbed, taking the Band-Aid from him. I put that Disney princess design right on his cut, pressing a finger on each side to secure it. I did it slow, clearly bothering him but apparently not enough for him to push me away. Heavy arms brought me closer to the heat between his legs, his eyes closing as he rubbed me against him. He was hard and touched his mouth to my blouse.

"What happened?" I asked, pushing my fingers into blond hair that smelled so good. I buried my face in it. "At the Sheriff's office?"

Clearly killing the mood, Royal tossed his head back, smoothing his hands over my bottom when he settled back into the couch. "Mira. I guess she mentioned me in her suicide letter. Her dad found it this morning. It was in an envelope on his desk. He said he must have missed it since he's always got a bunch of shit on it."

"What did it say?" I moved my legs, no longer straddling him when I sat on his lap. He let me, holding me to him with strong arms.

"Only that she was sad," he said, frowning. "That she was in love with me, but I made her life miserable. That's ironic as fuck since she made my life miserable. She was manipulative and tried to use what she knew about the haze to ruin my life. I told you why I gave in to her."

To push me away, the only reason. I looped my arms around his neck. "Why would she say that?"

He sat with that, irises flickering up. "I guess to ruin me even in death. The last thing she said before she died to me was I'd regret leaving her."

Had she meant that? Killed herself really over him? It was so sick, sad. I swallowed. "Why did you have her cell phone?"

"I didn't." He wrestled fingers through his dusky blond locks. "She must have put it there, wanting to beef up the letter or something. Anyway, it was evidence enough for them to bring me in. They couldn't charge me with anything because I didn't do anything. They had to let me go and did once my dad showed up. They gave me a call. I decided to use it on him since I didn't know what I was dealing with. I'm regretting that now, and don't you ever do what you did today again. Don't stand up to my dad. Don't fucking talk to him."

"Why?"

He tossed me on my back, literally maneuvered me underneath him. He pinned me down, and when he forced his fingers into my hair, guiding me to look up at him, my heart raced.

He was so beautiful, shallow breaths releasing from perfect lips. I touched one, and he kissed my finger, his tongue touching the tip.

Harsh heat simmered between my legs, Royal's hard length pressing into my stomach.

"He won't ever hurt you," he said, pulling my thumb into his mouth and sliding a hand beneath my skirt. He pushed into my underwear, cupping me. "And you make it harder for me to protect you if you do things like that. Don't ever stand up to him, December. Don't ever. Promise me."

"I promise," I sighed, trembling when he slid a finger inside me. He dipped in deep. In and out. In and out, and I rocked my hips up to meet his strokes. He only just had me on the brink of falling apart when a pound hit the door, both of us jumping. The knock followed three more, and next thing I knew, taps were hitting the window of the living room.

I tossed a head back into the couch the same time Royal looked up, and what did we get? Jax's fucking grin staring at us through my dad's window.

"They're in here, guys," he said, waving both Knight and LJ over. Jax's grin widened. "And they're basically fucking."

Once Royal had gotten off me—and removed his hand from my panties—we got ourselves together enough to open the door and let the cockblockers inside my dad's house. They came casually, sans uniforms unlike Royal and myself. They must have gone home to change, and the only reason I let them inside was because I happened to get a call from my dad basically as they came in. He said he was going to be working late, but he wanted to make sure I had the alarm system on, something I had the guys check after I got off the phone. With everything going on in this town, it didn't hurt to have some added security, I guess, and the boys not only checked that but double-checked. They were apparently with my dad on this, and after they got the place locked down like Fort Knox, they immediately moved into raiding my dad's fridge.

"Dude! He's got chocolate milk!" Jax proclaimed, then frowned at me. "Sorry, December."

I shrugged. Just because I didn't drink milk didn't mean they couldn't. The boys quickly got their bounty, and soon, we were back on the couch, me in Royal's lap while he explained again what went down at the sheriff's station. The guys all thought what happened was bullshit—which it was —and even more so when Royal's father came into the picture.

"One day that fucker is going to get what's coming to him," Jax stated, regarding Royal's dad. He'd said it a little hesitantly, looking to Royal. Maybe he thought he may feel some kind of way about saying something like that about Royal's dad, but since Royal didn't disagree with him, I think what he'd said had been cool between them. This was a messed-up situation, and I was sure Royal did feel a little conflicted about all of it.

I mean, at the end of that day, that was his dad.

I had one of those too, and I got being conflicted. There were some times I really wanted to hate my dad and others when I just wanted him to be my family, *my dad*. Especially after losing not just my mom but Paige.

Wow, we held so many similarities there, didn't we?

Royal obviously didn't talk about it, but he lost a mom and a sibling too, and as the boys and I vegged out on my dad's couch, we all got into trying to relax into what assuredly was not a relaxing town. Maywood Heights held some dark secrets, a murderer most likely still within its borders and maybe even more than one. We lost an opportunity to go to the Prinze family jewelry store today with Royal's arrest. I think we all came to the conclusion that right now lying low was best for the present, and as Royal later pointed out, his dad gave us an opportunity since he was headed out of town. Apparently, he was going to be gone all weekend according to Royal, so it'd be the perfect time to get down to business on a sleepy Sunday since no one came downtown. In regards to tonight, the guys offered to sit with me so I wouldn't have a night alone in my dad's house. I wasn't alone. Rosanna may not be here on the weekends, but I had Hershey. I later brought her downstairs, but these boys I was quickly learning were very protective. I idly wondered if Paige had to deal with that too, but knowing her, she was most likely doing the protecting.

After the guys went back to my dad's fridge *for more* snacks, we were all on the couch. Hershey in my arms, I held out several movie options for us all to pick through for the night.

"Okay, so these are our options outside of my dad's political thrillers," I said. Dad had a shelf full of them lining his office, so I made do with what I had, tossing the three DVDs on the ottoman for the boys to root through.

Four mini mountains eased off cream-colored suede, but it was Royal to smirk at the DVDs. He pointed a finger. "*Legally Blonde?*"

I shrugged. "Paige's favorite."

"And a classic." Lounging back, Jax pulled large arms behind his head. "I vote for that."

"Well, I don't." Royal moved it aside. "That leaves *Space Jam* and *My Girl.*"

Knight and LJ immediately lifted a finger. "*Space Jam,*" exclaimed on their lips but Royal and I did something different. The words, "*My Girl,*" fell from our mouths at basically the same time, which honestly caused both his brow and mine to shoot up.

The other three guys smirked.

"Of course, that's the one you want, Royal." LJ reached out for the *My Girl* DVD, then slid it over to me. He relaxed back. "Might as well put that one in, December. It was like Royal and Paige's anthem or something."

"Was not." Royal threw a pillow at him and when LJ tossed it back, Royal picked it up and slammed him over the head with it.

"Doth thou protest too much?" LJ chuckled, boys way too large fighting each other off on the small couch. What was really hilarious was Jax was in the middle of them, getting a few slams himself and eventually, Knight pulled the pillow away and threw it across the room—killjoy.

Royal pushed his dress sleeves up his forearms, throwing his wingspan back across the couch. He shrugged. "I guess we thought we were Vada and Thomas J. or something."

"Sure did." Jax chuckled. He directed a thumb at Royal. "They were even each other's first kiss."

Now that floored me, and something I obviously hadn't known. I propped my hands on my hips. "Really?"

Royal rolled his eyes. "Yeah, and it was the worst thing ever. I swear I washed my goddamn mouth out."

"How do you think Paige felt?" Jax settled a popcorn bowl in his lap, scarfing a ton of what the boys hadn't eaten after they'd popped it. He grinned. "She went swiftly gay after that—"

"Shut the fuck up." Royal slugged him, actually getting on top of him and ripping his shirt a little. Jax was losing his shit the whole time, *laughing*, which I think only made Royal pissed off more. Eventually, Royal got Jax under his arm. He growled, "Apologize."

"Sorry, bro. Sorry!" More chuckles from Jax, but when they both smiled, I knew Royal wasn't too hurt by what Jax said. I still was surprised by the whole kiss thing. I mean, my sister was clearly gay, and after putting in the DVD, I walked over to the male-infested couch. Royal opened his arms for me, and after tucking me under one and cradling Hershey in his other, he rubbed my arm. "It wasn't a thing," he said. "We were a girl and a prepubescent boy. Had to get it out of the way, I guess."

Made sense, I supposed, but it was still weird. I exchanged my snacks for Hershey who quickly bounded over to my lap, sending my Skittles flying. We were all about to clean up this fucking house before my dad came home. The boys got popcorn everywhere when they fought.

The movie queued up, and we all settled in as the credits started.

Jax crunched on some Doritos. "Didn't that kiss happen at your birthday party, Royal? That one where your dad rented out a whole goddamn amusement park."

Royal smirked, dragging a finger down my arm. "Believe me, the showboating wasn't for me. Dad always likes to make a statement." He tipped a chin at Jax. "And yeah, it was my tenth birthday, but that wasn't the year dad rented the amusement park. That was my ninth. The tenth was the circus."

"I thought that was your eighth." LJ was dismissive about the statement, watching the movie. "The eighth was the circus, right?"

"Nope," Royal stated, reaching over and grappling a bunch of popcorn. "That was the tenth."

LJ lifted his head. "Oh, yeah. Right."

They all sat with that for a moment before Jax spoke again and almost got a foot to the face for it. Royal was really into the movie and kicked him.

Jax flipped him off. "I was just going to say the circus was the seventh. I remember that."

"It wasn't. It was the tenth. Now, shut the fuck up."

Reaching around, Royal shoved Jax's head forward, and I laughed.

Jax didn't, though, shaking his head. He pouted. "Oh, right. You didn't have a birthday party that year since…"

The credits had faded, and the movie had begun, but that didn't mean anyone was focused on it anymore. Everyone was staring at Jax, someone who paused right in the middle of devouring a chip.

I sat up. "Why didn't he have a party?"

True silence going on right now outside of the movie and absolutely no one was listening to it. All attention had shifted to Royal, someone who was suddenly bracing the popcorn with a death grip in his hand. Unfurling his fingers, he casually ate what he had.

"Because, uh, I got sick that year," he passed off, panning toward the flat screen again. "Too sick for a party."

"Really?" I questioned. "What happened—"

"December." The warning came from Knight, his head shaking. Jax and LJ had all but looked away, and I faced Royal when he brushed my arm with two fingers.

The beautiful boy smiled a little at me, a smile that didn't quite reach his eyes. "Pneumonia," he passed off again. "Almost took me but it didn't."

Christ, and how terrible? That was bad, but I didn't understand why things suddenly got so weird, though. Nor why no one was watching the movie anymore. They all seemed hell-bent in sitting in this awkwardness, then watching Royal when he stood.

"I'm going to get some more popcorn," he said, taking the time to pause the movie. He tossed the remote on the ottoman. "Want anything?"

Since the question had been directed at me I shook my head and Royal reached down, bending my head forward to kiss the top.

"I'll be back." He left me with that, left us all with that, and LJ kicked Jax.

"Go with him," LJ growled, and Jax immediately popped off the couch.

"Eh, bro. I need something," Jax exclaimed, traipsing after Royal, and once they cleared the room, I ran my hand over Hershey's head.

"What was that about?" I asked, Hershey leaning into my touch. She fell on her back for a belly rub, really getting too big for that with her size, but I gave into her anyway. I smiled at her, but the guys weren't smiling at all.

Knight frowned. "Not our place to go there."

"Go where?"

Knight gazed away with a huff and LJ put his hands together. The tall blond leaned forward. "We don't talk about that year Royal got sick."

"Why?" I asked really curious. "Was it that bad?"

"Pretty bad. Yeah, but that's not why we don't talk about it."

"LJ." Another warning, but this time obviously directed at LJ, the growl low in Knight's voice. Knight's dark eyes flicked in my direction. "That was the year Royal lost his mom and sister."

My lips parted. "What happened?" I'd heard a car accident, but what did that have to do with Royal getting sick?

Knight wet his lips. "It was a car crash, but you need to ask Royal about it. I'm sorry. It really isn't our place to go into details."

"We miss anything?" Royal came back into the room, Jax behind him with a couple of beers from my dad's fridge. When Jax offered, I quickly took one, nursing it while Royal and Jax got comfortable around me. Reaching for the remote, Royal started the movie again, and since he hadn't missed anything I wanted to detail in the conversation, I stayed silent.

I'd been the only one to miss something in the end.

CHAPTER
ELEVEN

December

The tone changed for a little bit after what was said during *My Girl*, but eventually, things mellowed out. I actually ended up falling asleep, and I was glad since the movie was so sad in the end. It was probably also the wrong thing to watch considering my sister, but since Royal didn't mind watching it, that's what we did. I ended up waking up while another movie was playing, and kissing my forehead, Royal advised it was probably time for the other guys to go. My dad would be back eventually tonight, and the last thing he needed to see were four large boys on my couch. He already wasn't too fond of Royal. Royal slapped all the fellas' hands, and after letting them out, he came back for Hershey and me. Helped us upstairs. I'd drunk a little too much, one or two beers I'd had before falling asleep. Royal assisted me by getting Hershey in her kennel and later, putting me into bed.

He tucked me in and everything, pinching my chin and kissing my lips. His weight hovering over me and fine smell around me quickly made me want more, and I opened my bed to him.

"Stay with me," I hummed, pushing his academy jacket off, but he stopped my hurried hands, rubbing my nose with his.

"Your dad," he said, the only logical one here. If Dad wouldn't be happy about four boys on my couch, he definitely wouldn't be happy about one of them in my bed.

Smiling, I slid arms around his waist. "Lock the door. He'll know I'm in here, then. That I'm safe, but won't try to come in."

I'd gathered a few things about my dad too since moving in here. He needed security in proximity, nothing more. The locked door would let him know I was home.

Taking that for what it was, Royal grinned, leaving my bed only long enough to lock the door, then come back. After tossing his jacket, he unbuttoned his shirt, giving me a show when he exposed his golden, chiseled skin. His body was absolutely perfect, and he wasn't shy about not hiding it. He toed off his shoes, then joined me in my bed, cuddling with me when he breathed kisses on my neck. I wanted him here. I wanted him safe, and there was no way he was going back to his dad's house even if he wasn't there. I supposed he could stay at Windsor House, the Court's headquarters, but I didn't even want him there. I wanted him with me.

I sighed when he lifted my shirt, then pulled it off. That left my bra on but when he reached around to pull it off, I placed a hand between us.

"Can we just hold each other for a while?" I asked, and that didn't seem to bother him at all. He quickly got in to it, covering me with his hard body.

"That's like asking me if I wouldn't mind air." He smiled, tasting my skin. He pinched my shoulder between his teeth before brushing his nose over it. "I love you."

I loved him too, my eyes closing. He kissed the palm of my hand and I touched his face.

"Things got weird tonight," I said, playing with his hair. "You know with what Jax said about you getting sick?"

It actually got to the point where no one talked at all, and I had a feeling that had less to do with the fact we were watching a movie. The veer in conversation had made him uncomfortable, clearly.

Lids fell hard over green eyes. He pushed a veil of dusky blond out of his face. "Yeah. And?"

Defensive, and that was his go-to. The boy was a vault, and I hated that he did that. It was just me here, and he didn't have to be this way.

"Royal—"

He pulled my hands from his face, then hovered over me. Gripping my wrists, he pinned my arms above my head, extending my body and making my tummy quiver.

"Let's just be together," he said, placing his weight on me and reaching between my legs, he got back into what we'd started earlier tonight. What we'd started but couldn't finish. I sucked in a breath the moment his fingers invaded my underwear, protests hard for me at the moment. He unsnapped my bra as his fingers entered me, and I knew exactly what he was doing. He was using me. He was using *us* and sex not to talk.

"Royal…" He stole my breath with a kiss, a taste, and that was all it took. I submitted to him.

I gave him what he wanted.

———

I turned in the middle of the night, by myself, and I didn't understand. Opening my eyes, I realized I wasn't by myself, but Royal had retreated to the other side of the bed. He sat on the edge in nothing but his boxers, his head in his hands.

Basically naked myself from fooling around earlier tonight, I brought the blankets up to my chest. Shimmying, I got to the edge of the bed, and when I touched his back, his head shifted my way. My hand came away clammy, sweat coating his muscular frame. I touched hot skin. "Hey. You okay?"

Royal's hand covered mine, gripping on for dear life, and moving, I guided his cheek to make him look at me. His eyes were completely bloodshot, red and dark-rimmed. "Royal?"

A silence filled the room, and I brought him completely to me, guiding him back with me under the sheets. Together, I held him close, and he buried his face in my neck.

"Em…" was all he said, my name in harsh and tortured tones. He hadn't sounded this way before.

"Hey, talk to me." I folded my fingers into his hair, praying to God he'd talk to me. That he'd let some of this out. Whatever it was, he didn't have to do this alone. Thick arms eventually moved around me, and seriously, I questioned his ability to fuse me into his flesh. He held me so hard, so long.

His lips pulled apart on my neck. "I saw their faces, Em… I see them all the time."

"Who, babe? Who?" He sounded so terrible, tears burning my own eyes. I felt so much pain in his voice. What the hell was going on?

Coarse fingers dug into my flesh, my boyfriend holding on for dear life. "My mom. My sister," he rasped, tugging me into him hard. "What the fuck? Why can't I let go?"

Why would he want to? Let go of them. "Why do you need to let go?"

"Because I'm a piece of shit," he gritted, his hands so hard on my flesh. He pulled me hard. "Because it's my fault they're dead."

He'd said something like this before, admitted he was the reason they'd died when his dad hit him once. He said he deserved it. But how? "How was it your fault?"

Eventually, with some coaxing, I got him to pull away, to face me, face this. His eyes weren't just lined in red but glassy, a shine to them like he straddled a thin line on the cusp of snapping. Maybe he was on the brink, these moments with me the only ones keeping him from hacking that rope clear through.

"I got so sick," he said, the swallow hard in his throat. "I got sick, and I was scared."

"Okay." I smoothed my hands on his face.

He gripped one. "My family and I were supposed to go skiing. The whole family. My dad. Me. My mom and my sister. Because I got sick I couldn't go, and my dad stayed with me. He wanted Grace and my mom to still go, though. Didn't want to ruin their time. He used to do things like that. Be so nice."

"Your sister's name was Grace?" I smiled a little. "That's a nice name."

"Yeah, it was." His tone hardened, his expression as well. He swallowed. "So they went. Went without me and Dad, but that was okay. I wanted that, too. Wanted them to have fun, but things got so worse after they left. My fever was crazy... I was only seven. I..."

He didn't finish, and I held his hand, feeling he needed that.

He closed his mouth against my skin. "I got scared, Em. I got freaked because I thought I was going to die and I wanted to see my mom and sister. I wanted them home with me and was such a fucking brat. I begged my dad to call them, lost my mind until he did, and he didn't even need to. He had it covered. He was taking care of me, but I still wanted more."

"Royal—"

"They died that night." The words shot through me, the tears falling down from my eyes but not from his. He wouldn't let that happened, absolutely shaking in front of me. His nostrils flared. "A snowstorm. They couldn't catch a flight in the weather, so they rented a car and drove to get my bitch ass—"

"Don't say that about yourself." I brought his head to me, forcing his forehead against mine. I'd make him listen to me. He had to. I shook him. "You were a child, you hear me? What happened to them was not your fault. You were just a kid."

"A kid with blood on my hands." He forced my hands away, gripping them. "And child or not, that's truth. I don't deserve to have any memories of them. I need to let go. I don't deserve..."

What did he deserve, then? Was it pain? The beatings inflicted on him by his father in result of all this? Did he deserve to have all the happy times fall away with their memories? This may not be true, but he sure felt that way. He honestly felt he deserved it all.

Things made so much sense now.

In a single motion, he was off my bed, but in a second I had his arm. He wasn't going to run from this. He wasn't going to *run from me.*

"Well, I won't let you forget," I urged, grabbing him and throwing my arms around him. His body shook, absolutely quivering in my arms. He was a simmering volcano, only two seconds from the brink of eruption. I pressed my lips to his ear. "I'm going to make you hold on to them, you hear me? You're going to keep every moment, every feeling, because I won't let you forget the good things. I refuse."

An ache rumbled deep within him, his hard chest pressed against mine. "I can't."

"You can." I pulled him away, making him look at me. "You don't deserve the beatings. You don't deserve the pain from your dad and all this guilt. Your sister and mom loved you, and I didn't know them, but if they saw what you were doing now, Royal... How you were trying to let go of them because you feel like you deserve it..."

He blinked, his face so cloudy because I was crying. Actual sobs coming from my throat. I couldn't breathe, and something told me he was having a hard time too, his big body shuddering for breaths.

"It'd hurt them, Royal." In the end, he touched me, curling a finger and catching my tears. I shook my head. "It'd pain them so much. Don't you love them?"

"I do," he said, the words light and barely heard. They were filled to the brink with emotion and he gazed away.

I brought him back with a touch. "Then you can't forget. Who will remember the good things if you don't?"

His dad? The man was already lost to his anger, his hate clearly. I mean, look what he did and was still doing to his son? Royal said he used to be so nice. Maybe even like who my dad used to be before my mom died. Pain brought terrible out in people, but he didn't need to be like his dad. He didn't need to be cold and unfeeling to the world.

He braced my face. "I'm scared. Scared to lose them."

"Then don't." I touched his other cheek. "Forgive yourself. Heal and be free. There's no space for them if you don't release all this you have pent up and let them through. They'll leave, and you don't want that."

"I don't." Agony laced his shaken words, and I pulled my arms around him, tugged him into me.

"I won't let you forget them," I told him, holding him close. "You won't."

"Promise?" His hands curled into my skin, his mouth in my hair. "I don't want to forget."

Then he won't. He'd get through this pain. He'd let everything but what truly mattered—his sister and his mom—go, and I'd made sure of that.

I'd promise him that.

CHAPTER
TWELVE

December

My night was filled with lots of tears. Mostly on my end as I finally got Royal to open up and see the truth. Together, we got him to see *his* truth. He'd been blinded for so long. He'd been in the depths of so much pain both physical and mental. His dad had kept him there, but he wouldn't anymore. I'd love Royal as harshly and beautifully as he deserved to be loved, with as harsh and beautiful as I knew he loved me. I'd do that, and I'd keep doing it over and over again. Lather, rise, repeat. I'd do it until it sunk in.

I'd do that forever.

We held hands together on a Sunday morning, sitting in his car in the middle of a quiet street. With all downtown businesses closed, it was the perfect time to visit his dad's jewelry store, end this. I knew that cell phone was somewhere inside that store. I just had a feeling. Eventually, we weren't alone anymore when another car pulled up right behind us. We parked down the street, discrete. Royal started to let go of my hand, but I held on, kissing it.

Something passed between us as we stared at each other, something deep. I think, for the pair of us, something had changed over these past few days. There was no more me. There was no more Royal Prinze. We were Em and Royal now. We were Royal and Em forever, and I think he saw that too, bending my head forward. He kissed me, whispering words of love before getting out of the car. He told me to wait in the car for a second, and I watched as he walked in his low-sitting jeans to the car parked behind us. He bent his big body and spoke to the person inside, Jax the driver. I could see his friend well through the windshield, but noticed he was very much alone. I assumed LJ and Knight would be here as well.

Seeing me, Jax waved a hand from behind the steering wheel, and I did the same. They spoke for a second, but when my phone buzzed, I broke off from the distant conversation.

Ramses: What's up, 'Zona? I'm coming home next week, but I thought I'd check in. Haven't talked to you in a while. You ghostin' me again? ;)

I actually hadn't been. At least not on purpose. Oddly enough, I'd barely even noticed I hadn't seen Ramses since well before Mira's funeral. I supposed I had other things on my mind.

I snuck a glance into the rearview mirror, Royal and Jax still talking. We'd parked a few blocks away from the jewelry store so we wouldn't be on the store's security systems. Apparently, Knight was supposed to be working on that part, but since he wasn't here, I had no idea what was going on.

Me: I haven't been ghosting you, idiot. If anything, you've been ghosting me.

Ramses: Have not! My dad's been on this crazy kick. We're in the Swiss Alps right now. Can you believe that? Took me on a mini holiday.

Me: Wow. Why did he do that?

Ramses: Seems he wants to hang out with me. Says he wants to do it before I head out to college in the fall and life changes. Crazy, right? I guess this little piece of metal on my finger has been good for something. I actually don't mind spending time with him. He seems to be trying.

That made me smile. Ramses had never said it, but I had a feeling a relationship with his father was something he'd really wanted. Why wouldn't someone want that?

Ramses: Anyway, like I said, I'm coming home next week. What's up? School still weird? Crazy about Mira.

School was still weird, but I didn't really have any time to talk about it now. Royal waved a hand, gesturing for me to come. After sending Ramses a quick follow-up text that I was in the middle of something and would chat with him later, I got out of the car, hunkering down as I made my way to the boys. We were in the middle of broad daylight, and I didn't want to seem suspect.

Jax eyed me as I made it over. "What's with that weird walk?"

I rolled my eyes. "We're about to like rob a jewelry store. I didn't want to look suspicious."

The guys chuckled, Royal too when he threw an arm around me. He pinched my jacket. "I appreciate the stealth, princess, but it's the middle of a Sunday downtown in a small town. Absolutely nothing is open…"

"And no need for the crab walk." Jax jabbed me in my side, and I threw an elbow at him. He dodged the swing, picking up pace in the opposite direction. A hand behind my back, Royal guided me to follow him, looking like a god in his well-worn jeans and jacket. I wore my big puffer coat, really ready for this chill to be over. I had a feeling it was close because as we walked from the street to the alley, blades of green were popping out between the creases in the sidewalks and poking out of flower beds. Spring was coming. We just had to wait for it. I *needed* it, some good news and any sign to show the tides were changing in my life. We just may have that today if we could find my sister's cell phone.

"What does that mean if we find it?" I asked, shoving my hands into my pockets. I gazed around as Jax proceeded to gain access to the building. He must have been able to swipe keys from good ole Benjamin, but I noticed he didn't use them at this point. On his hand, he had some codes, punching each digit in one by one.

"We'll cross that bridge when we get to it," Royal said, taking my attention and responding to my last question. "Who knows? Paige might tell us exactly what we need to know. I'm sure there's tons of evidence on that phone."

"Yeah. DNA?" Jax had the jewelry store door open. He must not have needed the keys. "We'll get it tested. Figure out who the creep is. Whoever was with her that night had to leave something on it."

"But if your dad wiped it?" He could have, right? I shook my head. "So much can go wrong—"

"But so much can go right." Royal lifted my hand. "Don't lose faith. Yours is all I have."

He'd said that so seriously, something in his eyes telling me he meant it. Who knew the emotional back-and-forth he'd been through before they brought me in on this? My hope may be all he had.

Vowing I'd be strong for the both of us, I allowed Jax to lead us inside the store, but as we crossed the threshold I wondered about the cameras. Wouldn't we be all over them? Where the hell was Knight?

"Took you guys long enough," Knight grumbled. He actually lounged *inside* the jewelry store's back entry, LJ beside him. A sheet of polished glass and a set of double doors kept them and now us from actually accessing the merchandise part of the store. The building resembled much like a bank in that fashion, multiple secure entry points that could be either locked or opened to the public. Knight and LJ leaned on a wall next to a keypad by the doors, but both pushed off after seeing us. Knight frowned. "I disabled the security forever the fuck ago. You got the keys so we can actually get inside?"

Jax, I guess, had secured the keys from his cousin, pulling them out of his pocket and handing them to Knight. With keys in hands, Knight immediately went to those glass doors. He put one into the lock, turning it but stopped after a click. Right away, he moved to a keypad, punching in a random sequence of code, and I raised an eyebrow.

"Um, so he's a hacker now?" I asked, and LJ's chest bumped in laughter. I shook my head. "And how did you guys get in here?"

"The same way you guys did." LJ chuckled, watching Knight in awe like the rest of us. "The first set of doors just uses a key code entry. Jax shot that over to us via text before you got here."

"My cousin is an idiot and saves his work code on his phone. Swiped it and his keys at family dinner last night." Jax dropped an arm over my shoulder. "He didn't have access codes for the store front though. The store has a two-code entry. His other co-worker has that."

"Which is why we have Knight." Royal moved over to his friend, smirking as the guy worked. "He would have cracked the back-door codes if we let him, but I figured we'd give him a break."

"But what about the cameras?" I asked, that's a pretty big freaking deal. Who cares if we got into the building if we'd just be caught.

"On loop." Knight stood back, another lock sound popping. There must have been two on the double doors. Knight opened one. "Did that while you guys were outside bullshitting. Come on. It's on a timer. We only have maybe a couple hours."

Astounded by Knight's skill, I allowed myself to be led into a jewelry store once filled with staff and people. It was empty now, of course, the glass cases covered with velvet coverings. I didn't know why I thought the floor would be lined with green security lasers and booby traps like in the movies, but today, it was just a jewelry store with dim lights on. The boys quickly moved us through it. Like they'd been there a million times and maybe they had since Royal's dad obviously owned it. My phone buzzed right when we hit the elevators, and Knight growled at me.

"Turn that off," he chided. "Some of these alarms are sound activated. I haven't turned the ones in the vault off."

Feeling bad, I quickly shut it off, seeing another text from Ramses. It was a picture of him and his dad, the two wearing skis. He really was in the Swiss Alps.

Royal raised a hand to Knight. "Lay off her. She didn't know."

"Well, that's not a good enough excuse for us to get caught, now is it?"

Royal sneered perfect, white teeth. "I said lay off her—"

"Yo."

Both men panned to me, my hands on my hips. I reserved a frown for each of them before shooting a finger at Knight. "You, don't be an asshole. I didn't know, and you do need to lay off."

Knight's dark eyebrows jumped the height of his face. He obviously hadn't expected me to bite back the way I had.

I faced Royal next. "And you. I don't need you to defend my honor. That's very nice, but I'm good."

That shot Royal's luminous green eyes wide and got a chuckle from Jax. LJ actually had to choke back his own laughter from sounding in the room, and I think we all waited to see what would happen next. I didn't tend to do much standing up when it came to Knight or Royal, so needless to say, I'd been surprised as fuck when Knight came over and *grinned* at me. Like legit he grinned, a full mouth of his own perfect teeth directed at none other than me.

He slapped a hand on Royal's shoulder. "I guess I approve of her."

My lips parted, actual shock stunning me silent. Knight took the opportunity to press the button to the elevator, and while we all waited, Royal nudged my shoulder. He grinned himself. "I guess that means you're in."

Apparently, it did. Who knew that's all it'd take? Knight had never been my biggest fan and maybe he had lumped me in with the girls these boys had frequented in the past. He'd found me weak-minded potentially.

I guess no more.

The rest of the journey required Royal, his own set of keys, and later, his DNA. He had to use a personal keycard to get us to the right floor, something he said he'd had since birth. He'd just never had to use it. That got us to the right place, and once there, he pulled out another key he had.

I felt like I'd seen it before, a golden key. Seemingly random, he put that key into a box, and after he opened that box put his thumbprint to the plate inside.

The vault box instantly popped open.

I think we all waited with bated breath as, pushing up his sleeve, my boyfriend reached inside the box he'd chosen. He moved his hand around for a while, but in the end, he came up empty when he pulled his hand out.

"That's my dad's personal box," he said, a sigh on his lips. "I thought it might be in there. He's kept valuable things there before."

"So what do we do now?" I asked, waiting. We were in a vault with no cell phone in the place we believed it'd be.

Royal wet his lips, and without another thought, he put that golden key into another box. He turned it, then did the same process with the thumb plate. That box opened too, and when he stepped away, he nodded at the boys. They immediately came over, searching the little box, then the next when Royal opened another.

Royal took off his jacket. "We search them all."

And that's exactly what we did. Royal had us search them all, each and every one as he went from box to box with what appeared to be a master key and his thumbprint. The bunch of us created an assembly line behind him, checking each box after he opened it.

Though I was told I didn't need to help, I covered the most boxes. We stacked our coats, not an ounce of fatigue as we moved, but as time ticked down and more and more boxes came up with nothing but jewelry and other valuables, reality started to settle around us. How ironic we could be surrounded by so many jewels and wealth and not find value in any of it? At least, I hadn't. The one thing we needed probably wasn't worth even an iota of the cash and valuables in this room, but that didn't matter. My sister's cell phone far outweighed any value that could ever be in this place. That we knew and was why we kept searching despite coming up empty every time. Every box, every reveal got us closer, so we charged on. We remained hopeful…

It wasn't until all those boxes were open, all those boxes were searched that we looked at each other. That we *stopped.* We stopped breathing. We stopped trying. We just stopped and even in the shock of that, no one moved. We just stood there.

Knight had been the one to break formation.

He'd checked his watch, coming over to Royal. My boyfriend was on his knees, rummaging through boxes we'd already checked and jewelry we'd already pushed around. My sister's cell phone wasn't there.

Try telling Royal that.

Royal pushed on, searching, and gathering. He had probably a couple million dollars in his hands in fine diamonds, pushing them to the side like they were coal.

Knight folded a hand over his shoulder. "I can't adjust the loop again, bro. If I do, it could set off a red flag."

We'd been here longer than the two hours. We'd been here many hours, and Knight had adjusted the loop and security a few times. He said he could get away with it once or twice. But a third? He said that'd be pushing it. The store's security system had learning science. Too many times would alert the security company and he'd told Royal that many times.

Even still, Royal searched the store vault box, Knight's words as if gone unsaid. Knight nudged him. "Royal—"

"We're not going anywhere," he growled, tossing the jewelry. He literally threw it on the floor as if it was nothing. Forcing Knight out of the way, Royal routed to another box at his level, doing the same when he tossed a bunch of furs on the floor from another box. He'd searched *that* box in particular twice already. Maybe even three times. Royal sneered. "It's here. It has to be. Something so valuable my dad wouldn't let out of his sight."

"Maybe he doesn't have it." Knight challenged. "Maybe this whole thing was pointless."

"Well, maybe it's not." The look Royal shot Knight scared me and made Knight retreat. Lifting his hands, Knight backed off, making room for LJ who took his place.

LJ threw his fingers through his long, blond hair. "Hey. We need to call it, okay? It's not here."

"You don't know that." Royal gripped on to the box, a quaking volcano on the verge of eruption. "Now, quit fucking around and help me look."

"Royal," LJ started, but I pushed through, my hand on LJ's shoulder. The boys made room for me then, and I lowered, on my knees with the prince of Windsor Prep.

I pushed my arms around him, quivering heat beneath my grip. It took *that* to finally stop him, make him see we couldn't do this anymore.

"It's not here, babe," I urged, the words harsh for me as well. It was like someone told me I'd never be happy again, that it was over…

It was over.

We'd hit our dead end, the end of the line, but the thing was I couldn't give in to the pain of that. My rock, my force of a boy, was on the cusp of breaking down, and *that's* where I needed to be. I told him I'd be strong for him.

He needed me.

He leaned back into me, his huge body gripped his legs, and he closed his eyes. He didn't want to hear what I said, closing his eyes. "Well, who has it, then, Em? Who? Where is it?"

That I didn't know, but it was pointless still being here and risking getting caught. I made him stand with me, sliding my arms around his waist. "We'll find it. Maybe Paige's ex has it. We both think she could be connected to this. We could find her—"

"But how?" he growled at me now, snapping at me. I pulled away and so much emotion lined his lovely face. His jaw worked. "How would we? Paige wouldn't tell me who she was."

I knew that. I did.

Royal forced distance between us, seemingly mad at everyone now. Maybe even a little at himself. We couldn't offer him anything, and he couldn't offer anything for himself. He failed, and we had too, but one would have thought it was just him. Nothing but pure, unfiltered anger simmered off him, and that anger we let him have. He walked away from us, even me.

"She left me with nothing," he said, barely turning his back before leaving the vault. In all this, I'd never heard him this way before. He'd had hope in his voice, always.

I guess no more.

CHAPTER
THIRTEEN

December

I'd like to say things returned to normal after that. Normal…
bullshit. There was no normal. Not in this town and where so
much had happened. There was no normal for me or Royal,
Knight, Jax, and LJ, but there was peace. There was a period
of stability after prom season and when the weather finally
started to change. It came around the period of when the
flowers bloomed again and the world let in the sun once
more. No, there would never be normal…

But there would be stillness.

There were lacrosse games. There was *lacrosse season*,
which turned out to be more popular than football or even
basketball. At least, in this town. No one showed up for
Birdie, Shakira, and Kiki's games during the winter basketball
season like they had for the boys on the lacrosse field once
their season began. As it turned out, the team trained
throughout the whole year, preparing just for this time and a
season that had the Windsor Preparatory Academy boys'
lacrosse team six and oh. They were undefeated.

They always would be with their current captain.

Royal led his team to victory again and again. I knew because I'd been at every one of those games. I showed up for him and in more than one way. I was there for his show on the field, the place he went to get out of his head. I was there for one of the few joys he had while putting away the troubles of the past. That's all he could do. That's all *all* of us could do. Eventually, we had to put our search to bed. Eventually, we had to move on and heal, and he'd taken that the most hard. He didn't want to let go, and though I didn't either, we had to move on.

We couldn't be chased by ghosts forever.

My aunt Celeste had eventually come down. She'd moved in temporarily with my dad and me, and crazy enough, that had been a positive change. It'd been positive for me, nice to come home and food would be made and a familiar face there. She and Rosanna were like a tag team, the house filled with laughter so much of the time. Rosanna even got some time off with my aunt there and my aunt hadn't driven my dad up the wall. If anything, the switch had been nice for him too. He was home so much more, many dinners where we would sit and eat together, and when Aunt C. eventually had to go back to California and work, *my dad* had been the first one to offer to help her get to the airport. He even hugged here there, longer than I ever thought he would. They were moving on, healing.

I attempted to do the same, watching from the bleachers while Royal scored points for his team. He had a freight train of muscle out there with him, LJ, Jax, and Knight always having his back. They were such good friends to him. They were such good friends to me. I called out to them all from the stands, waving, and on occasion, I got one back from all of them. They always looked out for me...

Oh, yeah, and one more.

Ramses eased across the field, only a full stride to every

four of five of the opposing team. He clipped one of the Knightwood Prep boys with his shoulder, sending him down for the count and allowing Royal and crew to breeze by for our side. After, Ramses found me in the stands, flashing me a little teeth before picking up his feet and charging on with the rest of the team.

I shook my head at him, still floored that he'd decided to go out for the team. I'd honestly been flabbergasted when he told me about his intent toward the end of winter. I mean, he fucking hated Royal, and though my boyfriend wasn't too keen on him either, the two had been surprisingly getting along and not just on the field. It'd been like my aunt and my dad in that sense, the pair clearly putting up with each other for me, but they had been doing that. Royal got over the fact whenever Ramses made his way over to our lunch table, and Ramses the same when he chose to sit at our lunch table. Ramses definitely had his own clique, still one of the most popular guys on the Court and at Windsor Prep, but he did take time sometimes to sit with us. And when he did, the two guys put up with each other, they *played* on the same team both on and off the field. There seemed to be a sort of truce after everything went down, and it only helped me. I'd missed Ramses, one of my good friends, and dare I say, he'd missed me too? He'd said he joined the lacrosse team because it'd look good on his college applications, but since he hadn't given a fuck all year about grades or anything since he was so far ahead, I called bullshit on that. I only didn't fight him on what he said because I did miss him too, the loser.

Smirking, I waved at him, calling out his name and clapping for him. We were up in points, and though lacrosse hadn't been Ramses's forte, he quickly matched Royal, Jax, Knight, and LJ in skill on the field. Ramses, though a complete nerd, was obviously a seasoned sportsman. He was a jack-of-all-trades. He was *good* and told me he'd actually had a few recruits come out for him at today's game. He was getting money thrown at him from everywhere apparently, and that only made me laugh. No one nicer could deserve it.

I stayed huddled with a lot of the girls this game, the breeze cool and filled with earthy, floral scents. It was so nice to have anything but winter and sadness, and I got even more of that when suddenly Kiki, Shakira, and I were joined by Birdie.

"I got in!" Birdie waved something our way, a paper in her hand as she scaled the bleachers. She'd been late to today's game for a reason. Her dad said she'd gotten a college letter from Princeton. Of course, after school the first thing she'd done was go home. She'd said she would meet us at the game.

Apparently, she'd gotten into her dream school.

So excited for her, Kiki, Shakira, and I leaped up, grappling her like a band of idiots. We all nearly fell off the stands, and at that moment, our side scored yet another point against Knightwood Prep. The whole crowd freaked out, which was so funny with Birdie's news. It was like they all cheered for her.

"Let's see it," I nudged, the letter passing between us. It was legit. Birdie was in, and we hugged her again. She'd been talking about Princeton for months, seriously her dream school.

"I know, right?" She had a flurry of brown curls in her face, pushing them away. "Ah! This is really happening. Dad says we'll take a road trip over there during the summer. Isn't that amazing?"

It was, and she immediately went into the details, explaining the scholarship she got for playing basketball. All the girls did. Kiki was going to UCLA, and Shakira got in at Northwestern. These girls were all making their dreams come true, and though I'd decided to stay here and go to community college, I was okay with that. I hadn't wanted to leave, not ready yet. I hadn't found my place in the world and didn't want to make any moves until I did. I felt something was keeping me here.

I gazed out on the field, watching as chiseled legs and muscular thighs charged down it. Royal threw his hand through sweaty blond locks, someone else whose plans were uncertain to me. After everything at the jewelry store, we hadn't talked about anything serious, his own college plans under wraps even to me. I think it was still just all too much, my mind still on my sister, Paige, more than I wanted.

I couldn't let go of her, even now. I fell out of the conversation with my friends, hugging an item that came with me to the game. My sister's journal never left my side, always there with me, and I smoothed my hands over the pages. I'd actually been drawing in it lately, my little squiggles nothing compared to my sister's, but I did like it. It helped me feel connected to her as weird as that may sound.

I studied all those pictures of eyes she'd drawn, the cute little sad eyes I filled in for her. I drew expressions to accompany them, making them human, making them real. I tried to draw happy faces at first, but they always ended up being sad. I had no idea if that'd been because of me or her.

"Oh my goodness, it is her. December!"

A wave and two ladies at the foot of the bleachers gained my attention. They were mirror images of each other, one wearing a nice blouse with a cardigan and the other in a pair of shorts and heeled pumps. The one in pumps waved at me, her black hair flying across her face in the wind. I hadn't seen Mrs. Hastings and her twin sister, Daisy, recently, but I waved at them back.

Getting my attention, Daisy grabbed Mrs. Hastings, known to me as Lena. Lena used to be my sister's guidance counselor way back when. Elena seeing me too, she waved in my direction.

"Is that Mrs. Hastings?" Kiki asked, the goddess waving herself. I swear the girl needed to be an international model with her height and lovely, long hair. All the girls around me ended up waving at the pair, obviously acquainted with them as my sister had been. We all waved for them to join us, and the twin women made their way up the stands. I wasn't surprised to see them here at all. I mean, the whole town came out for these games.

"Hey." I hugged Lena since she'd gotten up here first, then Daisy. "You guys come out to represent the king today?"

The king was our mascot, out there too in his gorilla suit. It was the same symbol that donned the Court rings and used to scare me until I wore one around my neck. It was Royal's ring, a very precious gift to me, and I hadn't feared it for a long time. Embracing it turned out to be just what I needed.

"Of course," Lena said, then also hugged Kiki, Shakira, and Birdie. I wasn't surprised to see them all so friendly. I hadn't known Lena long, but she really seemed like such a sweetheart. She pulled back from my friends. "How have you girls been? You look great!"

"Thank you. We're good. And look," Birdie squealed, flashing her acceptance letter. "I just got into Princeton!"

Genuine joy flashed across Lena's face as she eyed the letter. She took a seat between Birdie and me, smiling as she read. "Birdie Arnold, why am I not surprised? Congratulations, honey. What about the rest of you girls? I'm sure you got into just as good of a school."

The others detailed just how good those schools were, and each and every announcement flashed so much pride across Lena's face. Eventually, the conversation drifted over to me and my plans, and after I explained my intent to stay here and go to community college, Lena bumped my shoulder. "Don't sound like that. That's completely fine too. You'll get a great education, and when you transfer, schools will be clamoring for you. My sister and I both attended community college before transferring."

"Yeah, even though only one of us finished," Daisy stated,

but did say it with a laugh. She'd sat on my other side, and Lena reached over and pinched her.

"That's because you were completely in love with the school's quarterback and decided to focus on that and ultimately stay here. Nothing wrong with that, Daisy." After she shook her sister's knee, Lena nudged me. "The two were basically married when we went to school here, which completely delighted our fathers. They were best friends growing up."

"Yes, they were." Daisy played with her hands a little, her faint smile to herself. She shook my arm. "Anyway, enough about me and memory lane. How have you been? I haven't seen you at the Mallicks' family dinners."

Well, that had been a disaster the all of a one time I'd done it. Not to mention, back then Ramses and I had been pretending to be fake girlfriend and fake boyfriend. I shrugged. "Didn't work out between Ramses and me, but we're still buds."

I waved at him for good measure, and funny enough, he noticed me out there on the field again. He pointed a stick in my direction, and when Royal noticed, he elbowed his teammate back into the game. Ramses shrugged, waggling his eyebrows at me before getting back into the game.

I chuckled.

"Oh, glad to hear that."

I turned, facing Daisy who'd spoken. I noticed her staring at my sister's journal, those cartoon drawings that I'd finished. I shifted the pages so she could see better. "Paige did the eyes, but I drew the figures. Just trying to match what she put on paper."

"May I?" Daisy asked, and not minding, I slid the whole thing over to her.

I smiled. "Great. Aren't they? I mean, Paige's stuff? I'm just fooling around, but hers are so good."

Daisy didn't say anything, thumbing through each page. She smiled too. Though, I noticed it was a little sad. I didn't know how well she knew Paige, but the fact my sister wasn't here anymore would make anyone who knew her sad, I supposed. Paige was such a good person. So much stronger and resilient to all obstacles in life like I never could be. I hoped I honored her by adding to what she'd already done on the pages. I could only hope.

"They're lovely," Daisy said, but when she started to pass the journal back to me, she hesitated. "Mind if I take a photo? I guess I'm sentimental. I knew Paige. Well, way back when."

Of course I hadn't minded it, and it felt kind of good that someone cared about what I'd done too. As Daisy reached into her handbag and got her phone, I gazed up, noticing we scored again. The crowd was on their feet...

And my boyfriend was being lifted from the field.

Knight and Jax had Royal up on their shoulders, LJ, Ramses and the rest of the team hollering behind them. They'd won the game, cheering, but Royal, his eyes were only in my direction. He lifted a hand to me, and I raised mine back, finding it crazy out of all this he noticed me. His team around and beneath him, they shook his attention back their way, but they couldn't take that moment from us we'd shared. It was ours.

Smiling, everyone else was up around me and celebrating too, everyone but Daisy. She was still looking at my sister's drawings. She had her hand over the eyes. She must have really liked them.

CHAPTER
FOURTEEN

December

After the game, some of us waited inside the school for the lacrosse guys to shower up, then take us all out. It'd become a thing for a bunch of us to go to a local diner on the other side of town, and since we won from what I understood was a big game today, there was definitely something to celebrate. I waited with Birdie, Kiki, Shakira, and some of our other guy and girl friends, heavily anticipating Royal. He'd shined like a rock star today, always did. Honestly, some days I really couldn't believe I was with him, but not because he was popular or ruled the school. I couldn't believe it because of who he was, someone so extraordinary. His light shined more and more every day as the dust started to settle around us, and I hoped in the future maybe we could all move on from the torture of this place. What happened mere months ago was a lot, and though I was still healing too, I hoped eventually, we'd all feel a semblance of whole again.

Some other friends who'd been at the game joined our small party in the hallway, and Birdie immediately went into showing the new arrivals her Princeton acceptance letter. I was so stinkin' proud of her and definitely gave her the floor when our friends crowded in and looked over her letter with her. In my step back, I played around on my phone.

"I'm sorry, Leo. I'm just... I'm sorry."

I turned, gazing over my shoulder at of all people Daisy. A designer bag on her arm, she came out of the headmaster's office, and Principal Hastings was right behind her. Honestly, I was surprised he even came to these things, lacrosse games. Maybe since they were such a big deal around this place, it was required in his salary or something. He didn't seem like the "social" type, but there he was, his hands in his pockets and expression grim.

He crossed distance to her. "Daisy..."

She stepped back, her hand raised. "I'm sorry. It's just not fair... not fair to them."

Immediately, Daisy left the hall in the opposite direction, head down as she put more space between her and Principal Hastings. All that none of my business, I started to look away too, but not before catching the eye of the headmaster.

He stared at me, that frown deepening. We actually weren't really supposed to be milling about in the school on game days, but not only did Principal Hastings not say anything when he noticed my friends and me, he just let us be. Severing our gazes, the headmaster stalked right back in his office, and when he slammed the door, I think I was the only one who noticed. Everyone else was still crowded around Birdie and her news.

Too weird.

That man was *so* weird and definitely wouldn't be missed by me. He was one person that I could very much leave behind and not miss a bit. Shaking my head, I went back to my friends.

"The champs have arrived!"

I rolled my eyes, knowing the voice of a certain Mallick

lacrosse player right away. Pocketing my device, I watched the crowd's attention shift to the end of the hallway, and as predicted, Ramses strode down it, his expansive wingspan wide. He pumped the air. "We owned this shit today, baby. Whoo!"

Typical bro and really falling into the whole "jock" thing. He used to play basketball way back when he'd gone to school here, and I had a funny feeling this behavior wasn't a new thing to him. It only made me laugh, snickering as the crowd of our friends instantly covered him. He hadn't been the only one coming, many of his teammates behind him. I even spotted Knight, Jax, and LJ in that mix but no Royal.

That was until I did see him. He stood out, his lacrosse bag on his arm and his blond hair wet and fingered through. He'd just showered, looking beautiful, and when I waved at him, he grinned at me. He'd started to come to me when some of the other boys attempted to grab him up into the friend circle, but he eased them away.

Excited, I joined him halfway, and he gathered me up before I could get to him, swinging me around the hallway.

"Did you see that last play, princess?" he asked, placing me down before kissing me. He placed his hands on my cheeks and everything, grinning at me as he warmed my mouth. "It was awesome, right?"

It was awesome, everything he did was. I pushed my arms around his neck. "You did amazing. All of you guys."

He pinched my blouse. "It's like you're paid to say that."

Not really. He had done a good job. He slid strong arms around my waist, rocking me, and when Ramses chanted, "We need milkshakes!" down the hall, I knew that's where this post-celebration was headed to next.

———

We ended up mellowing down at Friars, a cute little place on the north side of town. It was quaint and definitely the team's spot for after their games. The whole place was packed since the staff did a "winner's special" for anyone that came in during game day. The plate consisted of a burger, fries, and of course, milkshakes for a quarter of the price, so our table was filled to the brim with stacks and stacks of plates. These boys definitely liked to eat after they played, and it was quite disgusting watching Jax eat. He threw down like five burgers before he even touched the rest of his food.

Under Royal's arm, I watched his friend with a curled lip, he and of all people, Ramses, actually challenging each other for how many plates they could throw down. Funny enough, Ramses was holding his own considering how lanky he was, and color me surprised when he *won* the eat-off. The champ for the day, Ramses shot up from the booth, the room crying out his name.

Grunting, Jax tossed his half-eaten burger back on his plate, but did give Ramses props when he pounded his fist. The whole thing had both Royal and me shaking our heads.

Ramses eased out of the booth. "I need napkins." He pointed at me. "'Zona, you need anything?"

I rolled my eyes, telling him no before laughing at his dumb ass. Shrugging, he pounded *my* fist before going up to the bar and sweet-talking the server. Of course, she gave him what he wanted and then some, giving him stacks and stacks of napkins. Royal arched his neck back, smirking at the display. "Idiot."

He'd said this but smiled to himself a little after the smirk. Something was definitely happening between those two, and I noticed it more and more every time it did. I pushed his chest. "Admit it. You're starting to like him."

"I tolerate him," he stated, blond eyebrows jumping before he popped a French fry into his mouth. He smacked a kiss on my cheek. "And I do that only for you."

He had put up with Ramses invading his space. I thought my friend had a death wish for even suggesting going out for the team, but not only had he followed through, he'd done well and Royal, God love him, had actually let him. I'd be naive in saying the latter had nothing to do with me though.

Crossing my legs, I watched my boyfriend eat his fries, engaging in conversation with Ramses when he handed *Royal* a napkin. The two tapped fists, and even Knight talked to Ramses a bit, smiling too. Again, something was changing around here.

Something was healing around here.

I sat quiet and enjoyed it, the evening a good one. We stayed at the diner late into the hour, and I think Royal and I only left early because he said he wanted to take me somewhere. Needless to say, I hadn't fought him much. These spring evenings were doing us so much good, and I enjoyed them each and every time, the calm breeze and light winds. It reminded me so much of LA.

We sat in his car outside my house later that night, the lights on. My dad was in and flicked the blinds every time Royal decided to get even remotely close to me. Each time he got caught, Royal would just wave his fingers at him before returning to his seat. Only then would my dad be satisfied enough to let go of the blinds. Dear ole Dad had taken up with waiting for me to get home every night and had been very anal about it. For a while it used to bother me, but I had to admit it was nice that someone did care. It was nice that *he* cared and, as it seemed, did so without even being told. My aunt barely had to lecture him during the time she'd stayed here with us.

Royal laced our fingers together. "You think one day your dad will actually trust me?"

"I don't know," I said, sliding under his arm. I gazed up. "Think one day you'll stop having sex with me?"

Since that was not a chance in hell—on either one of our

parts—Royal just shrugged before kissing the top of my head. He rested his mouth there. "I want to take you some place tomorrow. You game? It'll require you waking up early is the only thing."

I sat up, eyeing him. "Where?"

"Well, *that* would ruin the surprise, princess." He chuckled, flicking my nose. "You wanna go? I promise it'll be worth your while."

Since he wanted to play games, I could too. Without answering him, I let go of his hand, taking my purse and getting out of the car. I started to walk away when I heard the window go down.

"Five, then?" he said behind me. I could hear the laughter in his voice.

Continuing to play my game, I stalked up the steps to the house. I'd barely touched one before the door opened, and my dad stood in the frame. That had become typical as well, him waiting. He nodded at me before peering a look over at Royal.

I did turn then, seeing nothing but Royal's smile behind the windshield. He waved at my dad, something he always did too, before starting the car and cruising down the driveway.

"You have a good time?" Dad asked, something he always asked now. Like I said, something had changed.

"I did," I told him, my phone buzzing, and when I pulled it out. I wasn't surprised by whom I saw.

Royal: I'm taking that as a yes. I'll be here for you in the morning. Hope you'll be ready.

CHAPTER
FIFTEEN

December

Funny enough, dear ole Dad actually hadn't minded me going out that morning. I told him I was going to breakfast with friends, and though Royal had breakfast when he picked me up on a Saturday morning, a few bagels and coffee, I doubted breakfast was the only thing in store for the day. Royal Prinze was being very secretive and wouldn't tell me one word as he cruised his Audi through the streets and later amongst the wooded hillsides of Maywood Heights. He went deep into the landscape, driving winding roads that didn't even have street signs. It was nothing but narrow trails as we scaled higher and higher up the hills of what looked to be some kind of nature reserve.

The windows down, I stared at the sights, waiting as eventually, we ventured to the top and above the trees. A wide abyss of landscape wasn't the only thing that was there when we arrived, and my mouth dropped open at the small helicopter stationed right at the top of the hill. There was a man inside it, one who came out the moment Royal and I parked. The man waved a hand in the distance, a handsome man who donned a pair of jeans and red leather jacket with his aviator shades. He appeared to be in his early to mid-thirties, and I had no idea who he was.

Turning off his car, Royal shifted a chiseled body in my direction, the sleeves of his dress shirt rolled up and cuffed on muscular forearms. He looked so sexy today I couldn't even stand it, his hair moussed back and wearing slacks that hugged his thick thighs and chiseled calves like sin. Flashing perfect teeth, he held his hand out for mine. "You coming?"

"What are we doing?" He'd told me to dress up too in his text he sent this morning, church wear but that we weren't going to church. The appearance of a running helicopter above the city of Maywood Heights *definitely* wasn't church, but I'd prepared for that anyway in a pink dress and high heels.

Our fingers laced, Royal brushed his lips on my knuckles. "Obviously, we're going to fly, love." And with that, he let go, taking the moments to come around the car and let me out. He appeared nothing if not debonair, so different from the rude asshole I'd initially met. We'd both grown so much since meeting each other. He pulled me to him.

"You hired someone to take us flying?" I asked, looping my arm around his.

He patted my hand. "Not exactly, but close. Come on. You'll see."

I could do nothing but that, guided over to the man I noticed now wore a pilot's headset. The man placed his hand out for mine, shaking it.

"Em, this is my uncle Addy." Royal pointed to his uncle, the man's shake firm as he released my hand. Royal grinned. "Well, Addison. Addison Anderson. My mom's brother. Unc, this is December. My girlfriend."

Royal's uncle Addy flashed a dazzling grin, just as blond and beautiful like his nephew. His hair was slightly longer, a snapshot of what Royal could look like in a few years. Addison stood back, gripping gloved hands. "Nice to meet you, December."

"Nice to meet you." Awed by everything, I moved forward as Royal guided me.

"Uncle Addy is actually the vet who took Hershey in." Royal leaned in. "Best in the city."

A boisterous chuckle had Addison clasping Royal's shoulder. "Oh, nephew. Flattery won't get you extra flight time. But nice try though. You ready? This bird won't fly itself."

What the fuck?

My lips parted. "We're, uh, what?"

"Just as he said, Em." Royal waggled perfect eyebrows. "I'm flying us through the clouds today—"

"With assistance." Addison raised a finger. "He's only certified for assisted flying."

But still, he was flying us? Royal eyed me, his frown slight. "You don't have to be freaked. I got you. I've done this a million times."

A conversation came to mind I'd heard before, one between Royal and his dad. It'd been a harsh one, but I remembered it. Royal had wanted to go to flight school, but his father had been against it, wanting him to go to a top-tier college. The conversation hadn't ended well, but that'd been the first time I'd heard about his desire to fly.

It appeared he'd been flying for a while, and it made me happy he seemed to want to share something so clearly personal about him. Royal didn't do that a lot, and since he was game to do such a thing, I would definitely be here for the ride.

I squeezed his bicep, smiling, and that made my boyfriend's grin widen.

Addison crossed his burly arms. "Well, it seems she's ready. Come on. I'll get you guys up in the air before you take over."

We strode to the chopper, Royal and Addison up front while I took the back. Inside, I'd been given my own headset to match the guys. I guess so we could speak to each other in the air.

"Ready?" Addison called back in his, and though I'd never been up in a helicopter before, I pretended to not have butterflies in my chest.

I let them both know I was and braced the seat as Addison maneuvered the joystick and pulled us above the hilltop. Royal reached back for me as he did, and that definitely helped keep the chunks down.

"You all right, Em?"

"Totally cool," I lied, squeezing his hand hard, which made him chuckle. The asshole found all this funny, and I shook my head, watching as Addison took us above the sea of trees and landscape. The sun had barely risen at this point, a wash of sunshine over the hills, and it was so pretty I did relax a little in my seat. This was just in time for Royal to let go of my hand and man the controls.

"Ease on into it, R," Addison coached, a smile in his voice. "Second nature."

And it was for him, nice and smooth. He cruised us from over the woods toward a city which now appeared miniaturized. The capitol and even the school could be seen from our vantage point, and I pressed hands to the glass.

"You're actually flying this, Royal?"

A deep chuckle sounded in my ear. "Yeah. All me, princess. You can see your house if you look close. We're coming up on it."

I sat back, way too giddy about spotting the colonial-style house amongst a thousand replicas. Dad lived in a cul-de-sac, a nice one but not terribly unique.

"Wow." I reached a hand over the seat, placing a hand on Royal's chest. "This is so cool."

"Right?" Royal leaned back into my touch. "I just love it. Love being up here."

Hearing that in his voice, I smiled, true joy in it. How could his dad not see how much he loved this? He'd literally struck Royal down for even the thought of allowing him to pursue a career of flying over general education. I supposed he just didn't care, the man truly fucked up. It all made me sad, and I tried not to think about him as we flew, as *Royal* flew. Our flight time didn't end up being much, but Addison did give us what he could. He had to work that day, some admin stuff at the office. He really seemed like a nice guy, and I thanked him for what he'd done and still did for Hershey. She still had daycare with him from time to time to visit other dogs. Usually, Rosanna came to take her over there since I was at school Monday through Friday. After we landed, Royal and his uncle did one of those handshake-hug combos guys do, and once I got my own handshake, Addison ended up peeling off in his own luxury car parked on the hill. He sped off in a souped-up Mercedes and his hand in mine, Royal waved him goodbye.

"I guess the men in my family love our toys," Royal said, pulling me close.

"I guess so." I wrapped my arms around his waist and he let me, walking us over to the now, stationary chopper. In the air, Addison had said the bird was his but allowed Royal to navigate it often.

Royal placed a firm hand on the red paint. "I feel like I've been flying forever." His voice held an air of memory, a smile to his lips. "My mom used to fly. Did I ever tell you that?"

He never talked about his mom, or his family really ever. I had a feeling it brought a lot of pain for him.

That didn't appear to be the case now, his arm pulling around my shoulders. He squeezed. "She just loved it. Grace too."

"Tell me about them," I said, gazing up. "I'd love to hear everything."

Some of that happy expelled a little, his expression tense. Especially around his green eyes. His jaw moved. "My mom was gorgeous. My sister... so alive." He shook his head. "It's starting to fade. What happened was so long ago."

I could imagine. He probably only had murky images of them now. The accident happened when he was seven from what I understood. I felt like I was in the same place a bit since I'd lost my mom so young too.

Lacing arms around his neck, I studied his face. "It's okay. And you won't forget. Not really. Things like today... it always brings them back."

Despite what I said to assure him, he grabbed my hand, his sigh deep and heavy.

"Why do you want to be with me?" he asked, truly asking. His lips turned down. "I'm so fucked up, Em. Might be forever."

Maybe, possibly. But then again, I might be too. We'd both had terrible things happen to us. I shrugged. "Why do you want to be with me? I'm just as fucked."

"Maybe, but you're gorgeous," he stated, his voice serious as he pinched my chin. "And I'm not talking about how you look."

I could say the same thing, this beautifully dark boy who needed something, needed *love*, and I needed that too. We needed each other.

He touched my necklace, well, his necklace, he gave to me. He thumbed the metal. "I've decided to stay here," he said, shocking me. "I got into a good flight school I can commute to, and I want to fly like my mom used to. I haven't decided what career track yet. I just know I need to be up there and here... Here has you."

He wanted to stay. He wanted to *be* and do that with me. He did know I was staying here. I told him my thoughts about wanting to stay behind. I wasn't ready to leave yet, something keeping me here. I think we both knew that had something to do with Paige, but that was okay.

"I want you to stay, to be with me too," I admitted and not hard. He's the only thing... *the only* thing I dared to let myself have. I'd lost so much, so opening myself to anything was hard, but he was something I was willing to take a chance on.

I frowned at a thought. "What about your dad?" He might give him resistance about this decision.

Royal's green eyes darkened. "I won't let him run me out of this town." He smoothed hands over my hips. "I'm going to be here. I'm going to be with you *and* Paige. He's bound to slip up, expose something."

And we'd both be here for it. We weren't walking away. It might take a lifetime to discover the truth, but we were here for it. We owed it to my sister and ourselves. Royal's dad could go to hell.

I'd hope the devil laughed at his ass at the gates.

CHAPTER
SIXTEEN

December

I was rocked awake the following weekend by Rosanna. She had Hershey in her arms and a worried look about her face.

"What's going on?" I asked, blankets falling off my arm. Gazing around, I was glad Royal decided to hightail it out of my room last night. He'd been coming to my bedroom in the evenings, escape from his dad and everything else. These days we preferred to be together more than apart.

Rosanna braced my shoulder. "Come downstairs, honey. Quick. It's your father."

My actual first instinct was to worry. It was the way she said it, that same worry on her face I'd seen before, so after she left, my dog still in her arms, I immediately dressed. With her coming in unannounced, I'd been smart to go to bed wearing something. Any other night with Royal in my bed, I would have been in here naked. Once dressed, I headed downstairs with sleep in my eyes and a race in my heart. I was actually worried that something was wrong with my dad.

That was until I found him.

He directed a man with a box, his business suit on. I didn't know if he was coming from work or going, but either way, he directed not one but several people with boxes into our house. The men and women in orange bibs moved around with our stuff, boxes... literally everywhere and at my feet.

I stepped around a few of the stacked boxes and even had to press myself against the wall a couple times due to all the people coming and going. I found Rosanna with Hershey as I made my way through the cluster, the pair of us watching my dad in wonder as he instructed these people where to go. He directed the majority of them outside of our house.

My lips parted.

"What's going on?" I asked again, but to Dad this time. The door opened, I gazed outside. There were more people with boxes and all of them were out on our lawn. There was furniture out there too, stacks and stacks, and a peek into my dad's office across the hall showed me the furniture had come from there. His office was literally empty, the hallway getting there. The framed art on the walls had completely been removed.

Dad barely glanced my way, plucking photos off the walls. They were ones of me, my sister, and our mom. He had quite a few of them peppered around, those warm and beautiful moments so long ago. Quickly covering them with newspaper, Dad fit them into a box at his feet. "There's been an offer on the house."

"An offer?"

Only a slight hesitation before covering another photo with paper. He tucked that one into the box too. "Yes, and make yourself useful. These boxes aren't going to pack themselves."

Jaw slack, I honestly didn't know what to do. I had no idea if my dad was crazy or I was just hearing things. I angled a look over at Rosanna who merely nodding, sighing before taking Hershey away. She mentioned something about getting Hershey her breakfast and that was when Dad finally gazed up.

"Don't allow her to make a mess in there, Rosanna," he said, before going back to his newspaper and photos. "We need to keep the house nice."

"The house… nice?" I asked, wrestling fingers through my bedhead. "Dad, are you even hearing yourself? What are you talking about, and when was our house even for sale?"

On autopilot was what I'd say he was in those moments, hearing me but not really. Dad dampened his finger, folding off another sheet of newspaper. "It wasn't. At least, not to the public. I put the word out in the neighborhood that I was looking for a buyer. That's how it works around here."

How it works around here…

"It's a nice couple moving in," he said, glancing up but only just. He frowned upon covering a wedding photo of him and Mom. "A nice family. They'll take good care of the place."

"And where will we go?" I stepped in front of him in an attempt to finally get some goddamn eye contact. He merely denied me once again, sighing.

"A hotel for now."

My brow jumped. "A hotel?"

"Yes, and a very nice one actually. Doesn't even feel like we'll be staying at a hotel. It has several rooms, more of a condo style than anything else. You'll like it. It'll be manageable until I get us settled in our permanent place."

"And where would that be exactly?" I folded my arms, waiting for some kind of frickin' explanation.

"The city." He looked up at me, finally looked up and stared me in the face. "Nothing's final, but I got a job offer up near Chicago."

What the fuck?

"I'd been looking for a while." Tossing a photo, he eased his suit jacket back and slipped hands into his pockets. "The offers have just started coming in, but I plan to move to an investment firm up there."

"And when were you going to tell me?"

A single eyebrow arched. "I don't believe I have to run anything past you before I make decisions, December. You are the child, and I'm the parent."

Could have fooled me *most* of the time. I grimaced. "You don't, but any decision *you make* does have to do with me. What about school? My friends?"

His arms moved over his chest. "You're in your final weeks of school, and I checked with the academy and you're on track to graduate. I'll make sure you get there for classes for the remainder of the year. And far as friends, you'll make new ones in Chicago. I looked into it, and there's a nice community college there. Way better than the one you were trying to go to here—"

"What about Royal?" My voice wavered at that, freaking emotion, but I didn't care. I needed to know about Royal…

I loved him.

If Dad hadn't shown any emotion before, he did now at the sound of Royal's name. Basically dismissing me, he ripped photos off the walls in quick time.

"You'll meet other boys," Dad chided, his teeth gritted. "Ones that don't leave a body trail behind them."

"What the hell does that mean—"

"You'll watch your mouth when you talk to me, and what *don't* I mean?" He raised a hand. "First your sister and then the sheriff's daughter? Mira? The whole town knows what he did to her."

"That's a *lie*. Mira was—"

"I don't care if it was. I'm not going to lose another kid!"

I stepped back, his voice never raised at me.

Nor filled with so much emotion.

Which it was, his cheeks several shades in tone higher than normal. With a huff, Dad bent, picking up the box he'd been packing. At the same moment, one of the movers asked if he was done and if they could take it.

He gave it to them. "Now, go pack something. Get together your sister's room or your room. I don't care. Just get something and make things goddamn easier for once and not harder."

Why should I? Nothing had ever been easier for me, and if it was, he'd never been the cause. I shook my head. "No."

"December."

"No!" I ran upstairs, getting my phone out of my room, then shoved my hoodie on. After, I raced right back downstairs, passing my dad along the way, before shoving past outside. He followed me to the walk, calling my name, but when I shot him a look he stopped at the moving truck.

"I'm not going anywhere!" I hollered over my shoulder, and as trivial as it sounded, he couldn't make me. I'd been on my own before, and I'd do it again.

"December!"

His voice faded as I stalked away, but I wasn't so bold to go back for my sister's car. My dad would probably stand in the driveway and block my path anyway. Instead, I found some stable ground and sat, immediately dialing Royal from a curb to pick me up.

"*Hey, this is Royal.*"

I breathed. "Royal? It's—"

"*Leave a message and I'll get back to you.*"

Fuck.

I hung up before trying two more times. I sent him a few emergency texts before going down the line to people who might be with him. I started with Jax and LJ, but after no answer, I got desperate and called Knight. He didn't pick up either and it took me all of three seconds after that to realize why.

Today was Saturday, and though I usually went to all the boys' lacrosse games, I didn't today. It wasn't a home game, out of town, and though Royal had offered to get me there, I'd opted out, not wanting to get up so early since the game was over three hours away.

I was regretting that now, picking up my phone again, and on a whim, I typed Ramses's number. He'd be with the boys.

He answered immediately.

"What up, 'Zona! What's the haps, kid?"

Oh, thank God. I stretched out my legs. "Hey, is Royal with you?"

"Uh, no." He sounded disappointed for a second, but only a second. "No, I'm not with him."

"What do you mean you're not with him? You're not with the other guys and the team?"

He said no again, sounding like he was getting up. "Dad got me out of today's game. And I wasn't at school yesterday for the same reason. Didn't you notice?"

A chuckle followed the question, but it was a bit dry, and since I hadn't noticed, I pressed my face to my hand. "I hadn't. I'm sorry. What's going on? Is everything okay?"

"Yeah. Dad just said he wanted to hang out. He got us tickets to a concert last night, and we stayed overnight. He took off work and everything for it."

Well, that was nice for him, but not nice for me. "That's great, Ramses."

"Yeah, it is. Everything okay with you? You sound kinda out of breath or something."

Probably because I was walking now, in the middle of the 'burbs in a pair of shorts, hoodie, and flip-flops. Distracted, I started waving my thumb like a loon. Like someone would actually give me a ride around here.

"'Zona?"

I said nothing, and when I whined he said my name for real this time.

"December, you okay?" he repeated. "What's going on?"

"We're moving," I cried, not able to hold it in. I squeezed

my eyes. "My dad's going crazy, Ramses. He's making us move. Freaking out and saying we're going to Chicago."

"The fuck?"

"Right? I left. Just walked out. Told him I wasn't going."

"Okay, okay. Well, where are you? I'll come pick you up."

I waved what he said off. "You're not about to leave where you are with your dad to come get me."

"It's not a problem. We just got back, early this morning actually. We just got in from breakfast. Tell me where you are. We'll get this figured out."

CHAPTER
SEVENTEEN

December

I swear to God I was the worst. I was the worst because I called my friend like a blubbering idiot, then proceeded to do the same on his couch for the better part of several hours. Several hours turned into all day, and not only did Ramses feed me, he let me gripe about my dad. I spilled everything, and around the third cup of hot cocoa, even Ramses looked exhausted.

Striding in from the hall, Ramses gave me that third cup in his living room, darkness settling in around his mansion. I'd literally been there all day and heard nothing from Royal. I'd called him several times.

"I don't need to bother you anymore," I said, tossing my phone on his couch. "As soon as he calls back…"

"It's not a problem." Ramses had his own cup of cocoa, setting it down on an end table. He looked so nice today, something I hadn't really noticed due to my own self-involved blubbering. His dark polo and dress pants were really fancy. Catching me looking at them, he grinned. "We went golfing this morning. Hadn't done that since I was a kid."

"It sounds like your dad is really trying." I folded my legs underneath me, damn if I'd spilled cocoa on this nice sofa. I guess I'd just add it to my list of bullshit I was unleashing on my friend.

Ramses threw long arms behind his neck, crossing his legs. He shrugged. "Seems to be. Anyway, I said the same about yours once upon a time, and it sounds like he's let a screw go loose since then."

The understatement of the year. I shook my head. "I don't know *what* is up with him. He's been acting crazy. You know he gave me mace? I think he wanted me to use it on Royal. Gave it to me basically right in front of him."

Chuckling, Ramses leaned forward. He braced his hands. "That's kind of funny, but can you blame him? *This town* is fucking crazy."

"Don't tell me you're on his side."

"There is no 'sides,' Arizona. It's facts. Your dad just wants to keep you safe. Clearly."

Albeit heavy-handed. I picked up my phone, but nothing from Royal.

"Don't worry about Prinze." Ramses lay back again. "Coach takes our phones during away games. Keeps us focused. Anyway, Prinze is probably showering up about now. Once he and the others are on the bus back home, I'm sure he'll give you a call. You won't have to stay with me."

I gazed up, really a shit friend. "It's not that."

"I know." His smile quirked right, actually touching his eyes. "I guess it's just my pride a bit. He won, and I didn't."

"I didn't know I was a competition."

"You're not." That smile faded, his voice serious. "At least that wasn't how it started." His jaw moving, he severed eye contact, and I did feel bad. Clearly, he had feelings for me once and maybe still did.

Getting up, I came over, setting my cup down on the table. "You're one of my best friends, you idiot, and I'd hate for us to lose that because *you're* an idiot."

The smirk bounced his shoulders, and I tapped his arms until he opened them up for me to hug him. That long wingspan fell around me, warmer than I remembered. God, did I miss him.

"I'd hate that too," he admitted, falling away until I was under just one of his arms. He pulled a blanket, wrapping it around me. "I suppose I'll get over you eventually. I hear Brown University has lots of prime college ass to get over a saucy little minx like you."

I'd forgotten he got into that ritzy school, the genius.

I punched him—repeatedly in his gut until he took that previous comment he said back, and though he eventually did, we both ended up laughing. I'd miss him. I'd miss these days. I completely planned on defying my dad and staying here, but Ramses was leaving. He'd gotten into a great school and was leaving like everyone else.

"I'm going to miss you." I tipped my chin, pointing at him. "Promise me you'll text when you go away to school."

Long fingers wrapped around mine. "I wouldn't dream of it any other way. You got me to come back to this place. Face my demons head-on."

I supposed he had, and now, he had his dad too. Mayor Mallick definitely didn't deserve any forgiveness from his son, considering the way he'd treated Ramses in the past, but it wasn't about that. Ramses being happy was all it was about.

Ramses and I sat there together before we heard other voices, pulling apart when those voices sounded closer. A door slammed somewhere in the house, followed by several steps in the direction of the hallway.

"You have to help me, Ibrahim." Principal Hastings... *the* Principal Hastings from my school stood in the hallway. He looked completely disheveled, hair askew and not himself, when he stood in front of Ramses's dad, Mayor Mallick.

The mayor slid his hands into his lounge pants pockets. He wore a bathrobe, clearly about to go to bed. He placed a hand on Principal Hastings's shoulder. "You need to go fix your marriage, Leonardo. I'm sorry. You can't do this anymore."

"You don't understand—"

Ramses cleared his throat, both men looking in our direction. Mayor Mallick instantly stared away, but Principal Hastings fell right back into that headmaster facade.

His jaw clenched, he moved his hand over at least two days of stubble before pointing at the mayor, his brother. "Then screw you."

Ramses and I both shot back, harsh words from someone who usually never said such things. Not once had I ever caught Principal Hastings being anything but a professional stick in the mud.

That didn't appear to be the case now, and I didn't miss when he cut his eyes in, of all places, *my* direction. I'd describe the look he gave me as nothing short of a sneer before he clipped the mayor's shoulder and left the man standing there in the hallway.

The mayor approached the open living room doors, placing his hands on the knobs. "Keep it down in here, okay, kids?"

Ramses sat up. "Dad?"

A question in that word his father clearly didn't want to answer, he merely closed the doors to the living room, leaving both Ramses and me sitting there with nothing but questions.

I raised my cocoa cup. "What's that about, you think?" I mean, none of that was *any* of my business, but it was too weird.

Ramses grabbed a pillow. "Probably the divorce," he said, and I raised an eyebrow. Ramses shrugged. "Sounds like Unc is going through one. They haven't told me about it, but I heard my dad on the phone this morning. Sounds new."

Ugh, that was horrible. I warmed fingers on my cup. "I wonder what happened. Mrs. Hastings… Lena is so nice. I met her at your family's Christmas party."

Idly, I wondered how someone so nice could be with such a stiff like Principal Hastings, but again, none of my business.

Ramses tossed the pillow. "From what I understand, he didn't call it off." He picked up the remote. Turning on the TV, he let some random movie play before staring back at me. He smiled. "Hopefully, they get it figured out."

CHAPTER
EIGHTEEN

Royal

I threw my fist so hard into Ramses Mallick's motherfucking door I nearly shot my fist through the wood. He opened on the third knock, just barely getting a "What the fuck, Prinze" in before I shoved past him.

"Where is she?" I bit, having been calling his ass for the past two hours. I had Knight, LJ, and Jax scouring the city for places the two could be. She'd called me, and I missed the calls since I didn't have my goddamn phone. I hadn't gotten it until after our away game at Kingston Prep, and after I tried to *call her*, she didn't pick up.

Ramses had been MIA as well, my calls alternating between both of their phones. The whole thing was sketch as hell, and this fucker was nothing but the opportunist. December told me how he'd gotten her to be his fake girl-friend so he could play out his little revenge plot on me. She hadn't said it exactly that way, but in so many words, I knew that's what was up.

Mallick wasn't speaking fast enough, and taking the initiative, I forced my way through his home. He shut the door behind me, stalking after me, and when the asswipe attempted to grab my arm, I shoved him away.

I directed a finger. "Keep your goddamn hands off me."

"And you keep quiet in my house." He got in my face, a bold motherfucker. "My whole house is asleep. *December* is sleeping."

"Where is she?" I got even closer, nostrils flaring. "You got two seconds."

We were in a stare-off, me and this guy. The dick actually had sleep in his eyes, looking tired himself...

Had he *slept* with her? I'd kill, *destroy* everything in his life the way he knew it. I'd end him with not even a blink, and I think I only allowed my mind to escape the thought because he waved me to come with him.

"She's on the couch," he said, my breath releasing a little. He scrubbed through messy, dark hair when we approached the living room. "We both were."

I lost his voice as I saw her, approached her. He had her curled up on his couch, blankets tucked around her.

I went there immediately, sitting with her. I touched a hand to her cheek, and she barely moved, such a heavy sleeper.

"She's okay?" I asked, cupping her face. I could breathe again, my thumb brushing her skin. "What's up with her dad?"

Her voicemails had been frantic and her texts the same.

Ramses joined us both on the couch, pinching his pant legs up like a little priss before sitting. He laced fingers across his chest. "Sounds like he wants them to move. According to December, he's been freaking out. Really heavy-handed with her lately. He seems nervous, scared."

Scared...

He had given her that mace, and maybe after losing Paige, he was turning a new leaf on how he was handling things. I thought the mace had been for me, but really, *he did* have reason to worry. Paige's killer was still out there.

I brought December into my lap, holding her. Her body curled on me, and I made sure she was held close. She seemed okay, just sleeping. I tipped a chin in Mallick's direction. "Where did you sleep?"

Like I said, the motherfucker had sleep in his eyes, and he rolled them as he grabbed a blanket from the other side of the sectional couch. He pointed there. "Over on that side. We were watching a movie. Fell asleep..."

"And that's all?"

"*Yes*, Prinze." Bunching the blanket, he tossed it. "She loves you. You don't have to worry about that."

I wasn't worried, but I didn't like that he was up on her, that she called *him* when she couldn't get to me.

I held her close, forgetting about him. Thank God that was the last fucking game of the season. I wasn't going to leave her alone again, whether she didn't want to get up early or not.

"And I guess you love her," Ramses observed, but actually hadn't sounded spiteful about it. If anything, he looked content, that he cared but not necessarily in an aggressive away.

My attention drifted away and back to December. "Thanks for taking care of her." The words felt foreign in my mouth, and I nearly spat saying them.

The ass grinned like a motherfucker. "No problem. Happy to help. She's my friend."

I did know that, that he was her friend. That's the very reason I'd thrown him a bone when it came to that haze. If I'd allowed him to get hurt, *her friend*, December would have never forgiven me, and that's one thing I couldn't have. She'd never have been able to look at me again had I allowed something to happen to Mallick, and that's something I understood early. It didn't matter how I felt about the guy. December cared about him, and I had to respect that.

He had to respect what I was to her too, what I'd *always* be to her. I played with the necklace I gave her, the ring mine but the chain from my mother. Her wedding ring went to me after she died, another thing to shove the dagger in my dad's face and lead me into years of physical and emotional abuse. She left me pretty much everything personal that held meaning to her, and eventually, I had her ring melted down and turned it into this chain. I wore that thing basically every day, my connection to my mom.

That was all the more reason to give it to December, my heart hers now, and I didn't regret that.

"I've been wanting to ask you a question, Prinze, and seeing as how you're here and everything..."

"What?" I glanced Mallick's way, more than ready to go, but I guess I would entertain one question. He'd been there for December, and I supposed I owed him that.

Mallick's chin lifted. "December told me how you sent her to Arizona. I'm assuming to get her out of this town, away from all this bullshit?"

Since he was right with his assumption, I nodded. "So what?"

"So it got me thinking." He scooted to the edge of the couch, his fingers laced together. "Why Arizona? I mean, did you even know anybody there?" He lifted a shoulder. "I guess I just find that an odd place to send someone, you know?"

It wasn't, not really. I brushed December's cheek. "I did know someone."

"Who?"

I gave him a look like he was an idiot, and when his eyes flashed, I knew he finally fucking got it.

He put a hand to his chest. "Me?"

"Don't make a thing of it." I shook my head. "I figured it

was better having her someplace far away where I at least knew one person."

"But me?" His mouth parted. "You hated my ass."

"Still hate," I corrected. I dampened my lips. "But that doesn't mean I didn't think you'd have her back if she ever came across you."

Mallick did some terrible things to me, some bullshit, but as much as he was a bully and an asshole, when it came to the few serious relationships I knew he'd had in his life, he'd been ride or die. He'd been someone one could trust if they were on his side, and maybe, somewhere in the back of my mind, I recalled that.

I shrugged a shoulder. "Really *don't* make a thing of it. It'll never happen again."

"Oh, I won't," he said, chuckling, then stared at December. "She'll never know how much you actually like me."

I panned to see a grin, one I flipped the bird at. No, she'd never know I didn't actually hate him...

I wondered when that changed.

CHAPTER
NINETEEN

December

A sizable weight hugged my side, and at the sound of a purr, my eyes shot open. I stifled a scream at the sight of a pair of jungle eyes and nearly fell off the bed when an actual tiger stared at me. It slinked its skinny tiger self in my direction, and when it plopped its weight against me again, it took me a second to realize I'd seen her before.

"Oh my God, you scared the shit out of me." I ran my hand down Dinah's back, *Royal's cat* Dinah, and the big sweetie fell to her back. She stretched out like an oversize kitten, not the mini tiger she was.

I grinned, getting her behind the ears, and gazing around, I recognized the room as well. Large, oak bed and dark silk curtains. They matched the ones lining the windows embedded in crimson-colored walls. This was Royal Prinze's bedroom, and if the sight of his room and large jungle cat didn't tune me in on that, the smell of his sheets did. They hummed of masculinity, reeked of *him*, and I basked in it while I rubbed on Dinah.

"You're going to make Hershey jealous, you know that?" I said, lifting her weight. I lowered her to my belly. "If I come home smelling like cat, she's going to seriously hurt me."

Dinah didn't care, a big ole softy, which was crazy considering her size. Jax, when he'd brought me here once, told me she was a softy, but I hadn't gone near her since her sheer size freaked me out. With her now, I saw exactly what he spoke about, and I guessed her breed was some kind of savannah cat or something equality exotic. Jax had told me this was Grace's cat, Royal's sister.

Smiling, I sat up. I wondered where Royal was, but not necessarily how I'd gotten here. I mean, I obviously walked but remembered being a little disoriented since I was so tired. Royal came to get me at Ramses's sometime in the middle of the night. He'd picked me up and everything, a true royal prince as he hugged me to his side and placed me in his Audi. He apologized for not getting my calls, for not coming to me exactly when I needed him, but I'd told *him* not to worry about it. I had a friend take care of me just fine.

That friend stayed at the door, watching as Royal and I pulled away. Ramses had waved a hand at me, pointing at me and telling me to text him in the morning. He'd wanted to make sure I was okay, and looking around, I spotted my phone. It was on Royal's end table, a note next to it.

The screen was filled with more than one text, one from Ramses, of course, about checking in and then about a million from my dad. He griped about me taking off, telling me he'd come for me if I didn't return, but since he couldn't possibly know where I was, I rolled my eyes at that. He was obviously serious about me getting back to him and, at the end of his rant, left me details about the hotel I was supposed to be staying at with him. I also got a few calls and a couple texts from Aunt C. as well.

Oh, God. He recruited her too.

Those two seemed to really be a pair these days. I brought

Dinah under my arm, opting out of texting my aunt right away to look at the note that'd been next to my phone.

Hey. Anyone ever tell you how goddamn beautiful you look while you're sleeping? Shit. My fucking heart.

Who knew I had a romantic on my hands, and I grinned, the note so obviously from Royal.

I didn't want to wake you, but I am making you breakfast. It's going to take me a second, so when you're ready, head downstairs and go outside to the back. We're going to have a spring breakfast like I used to do when I was a kid with my family. I want to tell you more about Grace and Mom. Out back in the gardens was their spot. I'll see you soon.

I didn't know it was possible to be filled with so much warmth, so much love, but this boy was getting me there so hard and so fast it wasn't even funny. He was a part of my life now. He was my life, and I'd happily give in than retreat. I think we needed each other, in so many ways, and whipping my legs out, I put Dinah on the floor, then grabbed my shorts off the floor. I couldn't find my shirt but found a very nice replacement to put over my sports bra.

I buttoned down Royal's shirt, the thing hitting me right at the thighs. I didn't even have to do anything pervy like take a whiff or anything. It just naturally smelled like him, and after bunching up my hair with a tie around my wrist, I led Dinah out of the bedroom. I'd only been in Royal's large Victorian house once, but it was easy to navigate considering the light cooking scent in the home. The aroma got stronger as I followed it down a grand staircase, the house's walls filled with photos from history. There were so many of a young Royal with his family it wasn't even funny and two others who looked so much like him. His sister, Grace, was his spitting image despite her red hair, slightly older but both held that same ethereal glow. The same went for Royal's mom, also a redhead and so lovely. Their presence allowed me to ignore the fourth member of their family, a father whose smile seemed to fade as Royal's mom and sister disappeared from the photos. Eventually, Royal's dad wasn't in any of the pictures at all, just Royal in his sports gear and things. His dad abandoned him, abandoned everything, and for a second, my stomach tightened that he might be home today. He wasn't my biggest fan, and considering all the obvious with my sister, Paige, I despised him as well. Something told me he was far away from this house today, though.

Mostly because I caught his son happy.

Royal's back faced me in the kitchen, a naked back with muscles that roved and striated beneath golden skin. He had bed pants on, his sandy blond hair tousled and perfect, as he rocked broad shoulders while he cooked. He had a song playing, one about sunshine in the morning, and I grinned, lounging against the doorframe. He had a grand display set up on the kitchen island, an array of fruits and toast stacked in perfect levels. Toeing inside, I snuck a strawberry from the spread before backing out. I'd been given explicit instructions to meet him out back, so that's what I was going to do. He looked so perfect anyway, really happy.

He was even whistling.

He did that to himself, no one else there to give a thought about it or judge. I found it so sweet, and after I left the kitchen, I urged Dinah to go in there with him.

"Keep him company, okay?" I said, patting her head, and like she knew, she walked that way. I smiled, padding down the hallway and finding my shoes. I wandered around a bit, but eventually, I found a pair of French doors that led to the back of the house.

The smell of sunshine nearly floored me, the whistling song of spring right in my ears. We'd had so many dark days before this, cold and harsh, but it was like the world was transformed and brand new. I didn't even need a coat today, pulling the door shut, and what a wonderland befell my eyes. I'd been through Royal's backyard before, but it'd been night-time when Jax snuck me over here. The boys lived next door to each other, possibly their whole lives.

I stepped down onto cobblestone steps, following the trail to a koi pond with active koi. They swam around lily pads with big, white open flowers, completely beautiful.

"God, Royal. Your mom was something." I'd been told she'd designed the whole landscape, large billowing flowers open and looking for sun. The whole world smelled so good, and within it, I found Royal's setup for breakfast under a willow tree. His mom had a large one right in the corner of the property, a table beneath set for two. Eyeing it over, I noticed Royal had a couple of starter dishes out there covered with mesh netting.

I pulled one of the domes off, sneaking a piece of melon this time. It was so fresh the juice gushed from my mouth, and I laughed.

"You don't deserve that. None of them do. None of *you* do..."

I recognized the voice, but wasn't able to turn around and confirm who'd spoken. A hand covered my mouth.

The bag covered my head next.

CHAPTER
TWENTY

Paige - age seventeen

It took me a short millennium to find Royal, and by the time I did, I shook my head. He was on the couch, beefcake surrounded by shortcake. He had actually two conquests under his arms tonight, the blondes hugged up on him like some kind of entree. Rolling my eyes, I stepped up to him in my kicks and an outfit way too good for the likes of this place. People were actually vomiting off the balcony. I frowned. "I'm ready to go. You ready?"

A spool of feathery blond whipped in my direction, my best friend of many years. Royal's arms immediately left the girls. "I can be. Everything okay?"

No, I wasn't okay. I was at this party on the other side of fucking town when all I wanted to do was wash my face off and take a bath. I shook my head, and in two more seconds, he started to get up.

Blonde on the right held him back. "Who's this bitch, baby?"

About to pop off on *this* bitch, I only had the thought

before my best friend pushed blonde number two off his lap and the other far the fuck away from him. He straightened out, dusting himself off like he was trying to rid himself from the sea of skank.

"This *girl* is my best friend," he said, crossing the room to me, then pushing an arm around my shoulders. He touched my face. "You all right?"

I was and didn't need his consoling. I was simply bored, and nodding, I let Royal do his caveman thing. He, Jax, Knight, and LJ were always doing that shit, a superman complex in all of them, but since I was over this whole goddamn night, I was entertaining it all at the present. I slid on my leather jacket. "Yeah, just ready to go."

"K. Just let me find the guys."

I was sure Jax was off getting wasted and the other two were getting naked somewhere, my guy friends a bunch a man-whores. I folded my arms. "You take one side?"

Royal grinned, the two of us of the same mind. He knew our friends as well as I did. He bumped my fist. "We'll reconvene when we find them. Keep your phone on."

I pulled it out for emphasis, shaking it as I began scouring the house. College parties were vastly overrated, and I knew since Royal, Jax, LJ, Knight, and I had been sneaking into them since we were fifteen. Even still, they put high school parties to shame, but tonight, I didn't feel like fucking dealing with any of it. I toured the house until I found myself on a balcony that no longer had anyone vomiting off it. It was cool out there, so I took a break to ease some weight off my feet and lounge on the overlook. There were about twenty frat boys down below, one of whom cannonballed off a diving board into the pool, glistening with moonlight. The guy crested the water, and it only took a squint to realize the guy who jumped was another one of my friends. LJ's stupid ass whipped his head out of the water like a mermaid, his long blond hair slapping his back. This gave the opportunity for two more blondes to float over to him. They quickly tucked themselves tight under his arms, and I shook my head at the display. Did I know my friends or did I know my friends? Of course, he was getting naked. I thought to yell at his ass from above, but then I saw Royal down there. He waved at him, and right away, LJ left the girls and swam to the side. Royal merely exchanged a few words with him before LJ pulled himself completely out of the water. The two headed off, probably to find the other guys, but it'd take probably another hour just to do that. Jax and Knight had a way of hiding when they had a good time.

Feeling a little stressed, I decided to take a moment and center myself. I had my journal on me, always did, so I set it out on the banister. I'd got the old thing years ago, something I'd thought was really stupid at first. My counselor, Mrs. Hastings, had wanted me to "write my feelings," but all that ended up coming out were these drawings.

The paper was lined with eyes, things that fascinated me about people. One could always see someone deep in them, no secrets, no lies. I found myself taking away only that element of people when I drew, and I actually took an art class this summer just to get better at it.

I worked on a set, a girl below capturing my attention. She sat by herself, fully clothed and drinking by the pool. I didn't think she thought anyone saw her, just sitting to herself. I loved capturing that, the moments, people in their most raw form. I got a little ahead of myself as I worked out the details of what I could see from here, quickly losing track of time like I always did.

"Those are lovely."

Hers were lovely, her eyes as they drifted over my shoulder to my journal. I'd seen them before, those lovely eyes of a pale blue.

"Excuse me?" I questioned, pinned in place, and the woman grinned, smelling like warm sugar when she graced my side. Gorgeous dark hair cascaded a face I'd seen before. It'd been a little while but...

"I know you." Because I did, the woman so familiar and with no reason to be here. I mean, a college party? What the fuck? But it was like she wasn't listening to me, her eyes on nothing but my drawings. It took her a moment before looking up at me and when she did, her smile widened. She pulled that lovely hair out of her face, tucking it behind her ear.

"And I know you," she stated, resting her arms on the banister. "From Windsor Preparatory, right? I used to volunteer over there. Worked with my sister."

Her sister...

"Daisy." I directed a finger, actually thinking she was my old counselor for a second, but God would that have been incorrect. From what I remembered, Mrs. Hastings was all sweater vests and knee-length skirts. This woman was wearing a skirt, but definitely not knee length. It stopped at the midpoint of her thighs, hugging them before displaying a pert navel. She also wore a leather jacket, covering a top that barely covered her midriff.

"That's right. Paige," she said, light and airy just like her sister's voice. Mrs. Hastings was always so soft-spoken. I recalled our sessions bringing me comfort because of that. She'd allowed me to say and be myself, and I nodded, folding my hands together.

"I was only on the prep team for like a minute," I told her, chuckling a little. I'd only joined as a favor to her sister actually. Mrs. Hastings said it'd help me, allow me to come out of my shell a little and maybe stop being so angry or something? I'd been really angry then, was angry now.

But that was neither here nor there, and something I was sure Daisy didn't want to know about.

I moved my jaw.

"So why are you out here?" I asked, unable to help eyeing

those soft-toned legs peeking out from beneath her skirt. She was fucking hot, mature, and definitely wasn't the type to be milling around a bunch of college kids.

Bumping a bit with laughter, she folded her arms. "Bribed to chaperon." She shrugged. "This whole thing is my cousin's party. Classic college kid. She needed a house, and I offered up."

"And what did you get out of the bargain?" I moved closer, and she noticed. With a smile, her eyes drifted away.

"Knowing where she is, I guess," she said, standing up. I noticed, too, she put a little distance between us. "She can be trouble. I wanted to make sure she was safe. What better way to ensure that than being around for her?"

Something not one person in my life would do for me. Well, besides my guy friends. No mature people in my life outside of them.

My dad was the ultimate heavy, and I couldn't remember the last time voices weren't raised in my house. I could never do right by him and probably never would. My dad was just as damaged as me, though someone would have to get him drunk to admit that. Where he took his pain from my mother's death out on me with words, I ran. I got into shit and was probably just as much trouble as Daisy's cousin.

In my silence, Daisy returned to my space. I knew because I smelled that warm sugar again.

"These are so cool," she said, really finding value in my drawings.

I lifted a shoulder. "I dabble."

"Well, you should do more than that."

She asked, and I let her see more, the pair of us studying my little dabblings. I liked looking at her more than observing her reactions to the work. Part of that had to do with how goddamn beautiful she was, but the rest, well, her. There was something so raw about her intrigue, genuine and thought-provoking. I must have not seen it when I'd known her before, so much more angry then.

"Can I draw you?" The words fell from my lips before I could stop them. I didn't want to stop them. I just wanted to be around her, see her.

Daisy glanced up at me, her eyes warm, but then some of that fell a little. She started to cover herself up like she was naked. She dug fingers into her jacket sleeves. "Probably not a good idea."

"Why not?" I asked, needing to know. "It's just a drawing."

"Is it?" she asked, surprising me. She played with her hair. "I mean, I appreciate you wanting to do that. Well, flattered…"

"So what's the problem?" I got in her space, maybe even a little too close. I wanted to smell that sugar, be around her more. My body leaned into hers, and I noticed this time she didn't pull back.

"I'm married," suddenly fell from her lips. She dampened them. "And you're like what? Seventeen now?"

"It's just a drawing." I eliminated more distance and, bold, pinched her jacket between two of my fingers. "What's the harm in that?"

Maybe I was stupid for getting this close to her, but it was just a drawing.

"Just a drawing," she said, but didn't pull away this time. "That's all it can be."

CHAPTER
TWENTY-ONE

The present

December

The jab hit my side the same time the car screeched to a stop and a second when I squealed. I screamed, bucking, and I was punched this time, so hard my face hit glass.

The impact shot hard heat right into my jaw, my head ringing, as I was told to shut the fuck up. I recognized the voice again, despite the bag over my head, hazing in and out, and fell to hard ground when the door opened and I slid out of the car. My hands bound, I couldn't help it. They'd been tied behind me at Royal's house.

"Let me go!" I screamed, a curdled shriek and so loud in my head. A strike slammed into my gut, and I bowed over, the moan falling from my lips. The bag ripped off my head, and my eyes fluttered from the sunlight, a face harsh and angry before me. Like the voice, I recognized it.

I just wished I hadn't.

Principal Hastings, *my principal from school* sneered at me, his eyes wild and crazy as they roved over me. He was a shell of a man before me, his normally perfect hair disheveled and his dress shirt untucked with a button or two undone. I think I'd done that, fighting with all I could at the house. I didn't have my pepper spray, not even thinking about it. I'd been merely going outside for breakfast.

How the hell could I have anticipated this?

I raised my head, my face and stomach searing from blows. Strands of hair fell from my ponytail, and Principal Hastings got a fist full. He jerked my head up, pulling at the root, and I called out.

He let go. "Such a waste."

That's all he said, such a fucking waste, as he grabbed my bound arms and literally dragged me across gravel. That's what was beneath me, gravel, as he wrestled me away from a black sedan. He had to wrestle me, all the energy I had forced into bucking and kicking. I wouldn't make whatever he was trying to fucking do easier for him, but since he had my arms, my fight didn't provide for much. He easily worked me over the ground, then up and over metal. Train tracks…

What the fuck?

I screamed again, shooting my legs out with sharp kicks. I wrestled at the zip ties around my wrists, so tight and digging into my flesh. Principal Hastings had kept his hand over my mouth when he tied them, keeping me silent while he got me secure enough to push me through the trees and beautiful flowers of Royal's backyard. He whispered through the bag while he'd done it, daring me to scream…

I was screaming now, the tears streaming down my face. "What do you want? Why are you doing this?"

He ignored me, muttering something, so many things.

"Always looking, always looking," he said. "Both of you always looking at me."

I had no idea what the fuck he was talking about, and when I tried to bite him, he literally grabbed my mouth. This accompanied a quick punch to my face, knocking me out enough where my head sagged and I groaned.

I choked, hacking, as he tied my ankles to the train tracks. He got my wrists next, muttering to me the whole time.

"The fire should have worked," he said, over and over. "The fire... Why didn't the fire work?"

"What fire?"

He barely listened to me, shaking his head and making the job he did on my wrists extra tight. His jaw clenched. "The fire should have worked. It should have taken care of all this, but he got you out. The little shit got you out."

My eyes widened, the tears blinking down my face. "You started the fire at the vet clinic?"

He shot me nothing but another wild look, all he needed to do to prove I was right. He'd tried to kill me...

What. The. Hell...

"You came for your sister. You..." He stopped, his loose hair whipping all over. He pushed it away, going back to my ankles to double-bind them. "I told you to stay away, but no. You and your goddamn sister..."

My sister?

He bound my ankles so tight I feared he'd snap them. I whimpered, but that only got me a kick to the kneecaps. I screeched and immediately weight pinned me. Principal Hastings pressed a finger to my lips, a rough, salty finger as he hovered over me.

My stomach rolled, on the cusp of vomiting, and his hand moved from my mouth to my throat.

"You're *making* me do this," he said, frowning. "Both of you."

"Do what?" The words shook from my lips, and his finger returned there.

He tsked. "I told you to stay away from Royal Prinze. That

he would get you in trouble. You're so much like her...
Always in trouble and putting your nose in things that have
nothing to do with you."

"What—"

He shushed me again, more crazed muttering as he sat
beside me. Propping his legs up, he rested elbows on them,
shaking his head. "The Prinzes... so elite, aren't they?"

The tears fell down the sides of my face, the sun in my
eyes, as I realized the open air and where we were. I was at
Route 80, *on train tracks* at Route 80. My sister died here.

Would I die here?

I closed my eyes, every ounce of my body quivering.
"Principal Hastings... *please*."

No way was he listening to me, not listening to anything,
but eventually, he faced me. He frowned again. "They think
they own the world but do nothing but cause trouble. You
should have stayed away from him." A chuckle curled his lip
up, a complete fucking loon. "He made your sister believe she
was a god. That she could take anything she wanted. That she
could take what's mine..."

"What's yours?"

Finally, I got his attention, and when he shifted on top of
me this second time, I believed I actually would vomit, right
in his goddamn face.

Long fingers folded over my mouth, biting into my
cheeks. "She was *mine*, and look what you made me do to
her? You're always looking at me, Ms. Lindquist. Always
looking..."

A finger drifted over my lips, and I shuddered. He
touched my throat. "Daisy loved me, you know? We were
together. We were in love, and I did everything for her.
Messed up things with my wife..." He gripped my throat,
squeezing slightly. "I did everything."

He leaned in, and I closed my eyes, his hot breath on the
shell of my ear.

"Your sister only stood in the way of that," he said. "I told Daisy we could be together. I told her I just had to leave Lena. She could leave her husband, and we could be together, but then your goddamn sister and her Prinze god complex!"

My eyes squeezed tight, not believing what I was hearing. I *couldn't* be hearing this.

The hand around my neck gripped tighter. "So I took care of it," he said, my breath leaving me. "I took care of everything, our obstacles... I *got rid* of the only thing between us, but it still wasn't enough. Daisy didn't want me. She'd been with your sister... she didn't want me."

My mouth trembled, my head shaking. "You... You murderer!"

The words didn't leave long before the hand around my throat squeezed, cutting off all sound. Principal Hastings guided my head over via my neck, his nose and mouth against my ear. "And you knew that, didn't you? You *knew*. You're always looking at me. Always looking, seeing the truth..."

"I didn't. I don't. I swear." And I didn't. Not until now.

I thought back to those stares I recalled *him* giving *me*. Every "look" I gave him, he obviously interpreted as something else, every glance his own goddamn guilt. He took my sister out and thought I found out his secret.

He gave himself away.

Ignoring me, his head whipped again, his crazy hair just as insane as he was. He didn't believe me, and now, considering the obvious, that didn't matter. He showed all his cards here today. He squeezed my throat again. "I really didn't want to kill your sister, Ms. Lindquist. I didn't want to. She left me no choice, and Daisy... I didn't want to do that either."

Either?

I struggled, those words repeated over again as he

breathed them into my ear. He kept saying he didn't want to do something, something having to do with Daisy.

Oh my God, did he kill her too?

That'd make sense, his jealousy and insanity driving him to the brink. If he couldn't have her, he'd end her too. Just like he did my sister.

"Please."

He responded not one word to my plea before grabbing my thigh, and I screamed, biting at him.

His punch hit again, my head slamming against rocks as he palmed my legs way too close to my shorts. He unbuttoned them, attempting to work them off, and no doubt doing exactly what he'd done to my sister and maybe even Daisy. He assaulted Paige, *murdered her* over Daisy and some fucked-up illusions he had in his head. This man was completely crazy, and here I was with him alone.

My life flashed before my eyes as I wriggled, as *I fought* with every fiber of my being. My hands and ankles bound, he got little resistance, my shorts undone and tugged down before he reached for his own. He wrestled with those for a second, and I closed my eyes, not able to look. I wanted to numb and disconnect myself from my body. I only opened them when a charged force blew Principal Hastings's body clean off me, a blur of size and mass ending up on top of him. Immediately, a round of never-ending hits rained down on the principal's face in a sea of punches. They wouldn't stop, and squinting, I made out Royal's big body in the sun.

A wash of dirty blond hair shrouded his face as he threw down punches at our principal again and again, the educator's face turning into mashed meat. Royal pummeled him with never-ending blows while his fists became coated in dark red. Royal didn't care. He just kept going, wouldn't stop, and in his rage gave room for opportunity. He didn't see Principal Hastings reaching. He *didn't see* him go for the gun that was positioned right at Royal's hip. It'd clearly been reserved for someone else, not this moment.

No...

The shot fired, and Royal's expression blanked, my shriek lining the air as the smoking gun clouded between us. I was that close to Royal, could see the dread and fear all over his beautiful face as he fell, fell beside me.

"Royal!"

Pistol whipped for my cry, I silenced, my eyes on Royal. His eyes were on me too, the pair of us in our own world as a shadow hovered over us. We didn't even look, only staring at each other. I wouldn't close my eyes. I'd only look at him, those green eyes if they were going to be my last thing.

Maybe Royal felt the same way, staring at me too. I had no idea where he'd been shot, but he reached for me, taking my hand. He threaded them together, with me to the end. I flinched when another shot fired, and I believed that was it.

That was until I saw the body.

Holding his chest, Principal Hastings's fell to his front, his face slamming gravel beside us. In shock, I turned to see a figure running, coming right at us and calling my name.

"December!"

My dad dropped to his knees, his phone at his ear. He was calling 911 with a gun in his hand, a smoking gun.

I faced my principal again, unmoved before turning back to Royal. He no longer had his eyes on me, his lids closed.

"Royal? Royal!" I attempted to move toward him, but my dad shouted at me to stay still. He didn't want me to move, but I wasn't hurt. Royal was. "Dad, I'm fine. Help him. Help Royal!"

He wasn't listening to me, on the phone with emergency. I had to lie there, stewing in moments of wonder as I stared at my boyfriend, who lay incredibly still on the ground beside me.

I didn't even know if he was breathing.

CHAPTER
TWENTY-TWO

Graduation Day

December

A lot of people didn't make it across that stage the day of
Windsor Preparatory Academy's graduation. A lot of people
had their lives stolen away from the darkness of this town,
and one of those people was my sister. She'd had an affair
with a married woman and that sole decision resulted in a
chain of events that I still was reeling from. The choice left
people widowed, Daisy's husband, the mayor's chief of staff,
included in that number. We found out Daisy's life had also
been taken by a madman, Principal Hastings's jealous rage
concluding in a way that not only left this town bloody but a
graduation stage filled with a somber mood. Someone else's
sister had to stand on that stage and hand out diplomas, Lena
Hastings left both without a spouse and a sister. She'd been

designated temporary headmaster until the position could be filled in the fall, the woman so strong. She stood there with pride as if she hadn't lost it all, her sister and dear friend betraying her. Who knew how long the affair between Daisy and Principal Hastings had gone on. It'd been long enough for him to know Daisy had been unfaithful to him, long enough for my sister to come in and get swept away in something she never should have been a part of. She ultimately paid for that decision, left so many of us behind, and Mira was also not present at this graduation. Mira, a girl I'd never been crazy about but who hadn't deserved to die. It'd been captured on tape what actually happened to her, the footage coming out not long after the dust fell, and the true horror of who Principal Hastings was came to fruition. He had cameras in his office, ones no one thought to check until he gave the world a reason.

The world got to see everything.

They saw Mira coming to his office the day of her death. She'd gone there trying to throw, of all people, Royal under the bus because he hadn't wanted to be with her. She'd decided to tell the Windsor Prep headmaster about the haze on my sister for not Paige's well-being but her own. She wanted to hurt Royal, going to the one official she believed would care and help her. All that did was alert the true murderer of that night. It let Principal Hastings know someone else knew about something that went down at Route 80. It didn't matter Mira probably knew nothing else, knew nothing about what he'd actually done in the end.

Always looking at me...

Mira became another set of eyes to him, a witness and another thread that needed to be closed. He'd strangled her, *right* in his office, and once that came to light, everything else fell into place. He'd broken into her house and staged her suicide, clear evidence of that after the video surveillance surfaced. He'd had all the means, her house keys, and the suicide letter even matched his own handwriting when analyzed. He'd even tried to set up Royal as the one who influenced her. It'd been him to plant Mira's cellphone in Royal's locker in the end.

Principal Hastings had been sloppy, careless and clearly unhinged, but no one had had reason to suspect him. That was the only reason he'd gotten away with things for as long as he had. He was sick, fucked up and twisted. He'd even kept Mira's house keys in a treasure trove in his home…

That's where they'd found my sister's cell phone. It'd been there the whole time with the principal's other tokens. He had locks of Daisy's hair in there, underwear. It didn't take the authorities long to find out what happened to her. She'd been found, dead like so many others, in her own home. She'd been strangled, another "suicide," and how Principal Hastings had perfected the art. The sheriff's office themselves even said they wouldn't have known the difference. Principal Hastings had been skilled.

Swallowing hard, Lena read off my name on the stage, handing me *my* diploma in front of a gym full of my peers and our family and friends. As she handed it to me, a sheen coated her eyes, but I was sure it wasn't for me. I had no idea how she'd handle things after all that had happened, but I hoped the best for her. She was so good, kind and didn't deserve what had happened to her surrounding the people in her life. She shouldn't have been married to a madman. She shouldn't have had a sister betray her, and she shouldn't have to do this today, but she'd at least chosen that.

"I want to make up for this," she'd told me that night at the sheriff's office. *"Make up for him and her."*

And this was her trying, being strong. She handed my diploma to me, myself the last thread who Principal Hastings tried to shut up. I wouldn't be shut up…

I had too many people in my corner.

I found them all out there in the audience, Aunt Celeste and *my* dad the biggest cheerers in the crowd. They both stood with cell phones, my dad actually smiling. He'd found me that day at the train tracks, *saved me* using what I'd later found out was an app. He'd snuck one onto my phone to keep tabs on me, something I couldn't even be mad about for obvious reasons in the end. I guess Dad had been worried the days leading up to my assault, and it'd been for good reason. It turned out his employer, Mr. Prinze, had threatened him to leave town, but not overtly. There'd been flippant comments made here and there, ones that put my dad more than on edge, hence his heavy hand when it came to me and my safety. Dad later told me prior to the comments had been more threats, but in the beginning, only in nonconventional ways. Mr. Prinze had bribed him, given him gifts, bonuses, and even a car. These gifts came with conversations, ones that implied my dad could find better work and Mr. Prinze himself would give a personal recommendation if Dad ever did. The thing was, Dad hadn't chosen to leave and that's when Mr. Prinze got more aggressive. He cornered my dad more than a few times at work, enough to bother him. Dad had no idea why, but it all came out in court when Mr. Prinze had been forced to testify for his role in the murder of my sister. As it turned out, the man did have reasons to cover up a murder, but that had nothing to do with his son.

Mr. Prinze found out Royal and the other boys had been there out on Route 80 that night, and obviously, that didn't look good. Mr. Prinze covered things up to protect only himself and prevent scandal. He was watching his back and only his alone, not Royal's. Mr. Prinze admitted the whole thing in court, his hands completely bloody. He got a conviction that day, along with several others, life convictions for Principal Hastings and jail time for the sheriff as well. He'd helped with the whole cover-up, the police needed in all this, but I was sure the man had no idea how far our principal would go in the end to conceal the truth. Had he, he wouldn't have bothered to help. The man killed the sheriff's daughter in the end.

It'd been a long and painful trial, but one of the sweetest convictions by far had been Mr. Prinze. He was told right there his entire life as he knew it would be taken away.

And he had to do it in front of his son.

I stood as Royal's name was called, our valedictorian. Would you know it, he had the best grades in our class despite being hospitalized for weeks. A gunshot to the abdomen wouldn't slow him down. He had me, Knight, Jax, and LJ and even some of my friends bring him his work every day. We stayed with him, supported him until he walked again and ultimately, out of that hospital. Even then, I didn't leave his side. I couldn't. I'd been so close to losing him.

My boyfriend had actually jumped in front of a bullet for me. I mean, who could actually say that? It just proved his loyalty to not just me, but Paige as well. I guess he did look out for me in the end.

I stood tall, clapping as Royal stepped to the podium to give his speech to our class. He wore the same dark robes we all did, but by far, filled it out in ways not even the average Court guy could do. His muscular shoulders framed the whole thing, fitted perfectly over his big body, and his blond hair was moussed and shaped divinely under his cap. Lena gave him a hug once he got up there, sharing a few words with him. Whatever they were, he smiled at her, so many smiles these days. It was like actual light came back into him once his dad was locked up and Principal Hastings had been shipped out to a high-security prison in bumfuck nowhere. Justice was finally served, and we all got to see it.

The crowd had calmed down, but I still clapped. I couldn't stop. He deserved it so much.

Royal's gaze made it out to me during my applause, his

chin raised, and I didn't care that only *my applause* radiated in that room. I'd still keep on, until my hands hurt. In my periphery, that applause was joined, and when I turned, Knight was there backing me up. His claps were boisterous, radiating in the room, and quickly followed by two more.

LJ, our salutatorian, applauded too from the stage. He sat with the teachers, Royal's empty seat beside him. Well, once he clapped, there went Jax too. He was closer by, closer to me. Jax whistled loudly with his thick fingers, and the crowd laughed.

I found my second wind with my applause still going on, and my friends at my sides joined me. I spotted Kiki, Birdie, and Shakira with a few of our other friends from the basketball team. Court boys popped up from various seats after that, and once they stood, the whole audience did, a shower of applause. They knew what Royal had been through, what we'd all gone through to be here. We all deserved the applause, this whole town.

In the middle of it all, Royal spotted me, and once it concluded, he kissed two fingers, placing them out to me. He pointed right after, taking his spot behind the podium with his speech in hand. Stepping in front of the microphone, I knew this was finally it, the last part of himself he had to give to anyone else around here. After today, he was free.

After today, he'd begin his life.

———

That mindset traveled with me throughout the day, the freedom and ability to begin one's life. I'd felt restricted and bound for so long by my own mental battles. They'd been powerful, and in the thick of it, I wasn't sure if I'd come out the victor. It took coming here to this town to change things for me, and oddly enough, the love of a guy to only strengthen my own victory. Royal inspired me so much, how someone could go through so much pain to not only defeat his obstacles but rise above them. Mr. Prinze had been the most powerful member of the Court, the president I found out. There were some very high-ranking officials, but an emergency vote lifted the youngest president ever named in Court history up the ranks. Royal was now president of his prestigious Court, and what did that mean for the town?

Well, unity.

That could be seen at the graduation after-party, held at none other than Windsor House, and no one had been left out. Anyone and from every walk of life was allowed in, and the House was filled to the brim with Court boys, Kept girls, and the rest of the town. Those labels felt so weird now, so much had changed. Even those final weeks of school were totally blended, Court boys sitting with nerds and jocks hanging out with chess club geeks. People didn't care about their labels. They were just being themselves, and how awesome that I could to be a part of that.

I thought about that as I mingled and chatted with some of my friends. I knew it might be a very long time before I ever saw them again. We were all going to go our separate ways after this, some college, some jobs, and other things. Today might be our last day, but all I could think was that my sister did all this. *My sister* brought us all together. What happened to her was truly horrific and something I may never get over. No, I wouldn't ever get over it. The pain was deep, and though I may never truly heal, I couldn't deny this moment and the warm thoughts that came with it. What happened to my sister brought an entire town together and provided a strength in me I never thought I knew.

"You hiding, 'Zona?"

I smiled before turning to find another friend, someone who'd greatly been affected by the darkness in this town too. Ramses's dad had been one of those indicted amongst those with crimes against my sister. As it turned out, Principal

Hastings went to his brother, the mayor, for help after the murder. He needed to know what to do and all of that came out at the trial. Mayor Mallick not only helped him, but was the one who went to Mr. Prinze for aid. Mayor Mallick knew Mr. Prinze would have interest because of Royal and the reason Paige was out there. He'd used that to rope Mr. Prinze in all this madness.

I think maybe the mayor knew things would implode the way they did, though. He'd been taking Ramses away, spending so much time with him. I was so happy Ramses even came out to party tonight. He opted out of the graduation entirely, keeping more to himself these days, and no one would blame him. He'd been through just as much as all of us.

My friend had found me out on the balcony, and I hugged him, the embrace so familiar. He was so warm, big and all-encompassing. In another life, we may have been together. He really was perfect, but I guess for someone else.

Ramses didn't let go of me at first, but not because he didn't try. I hadn't let go of him, knowing he was going to go away soon. He had plans to go to college on the East Coast, as far away on one side of the country as he could.

"Jesus, 'Zona. You trying to meld your way into me?" He chuckled.

If I could. I'd miss him so much. At least Birdie, Shakira, Kiki, and I had the entire summer together. He was leaving like next week.

I let go, then wrestled in his wild curls. "I'll just miss you is all."

"I'll miss you too." He held on to my hips, his smile full, genuine. It was one of the things I loved about him. If he wasn't happy, he didn't bullshit. He tugged my hair. "You can always come out and see me, you know? I'll pay for the ticket."

"Mallick, how many times do I need to tell you to keep your hands off my girl?"

Ramses rolled his eyes, but did let go of me. He threw an arm around my shoulders. "'Your girl' can't keep her hands off *me*, bro," he said, squeezing me. "I guess I don't blame her. I am pretty awesome."

From the balcony doors, Royal rushed like a juggernaut in our direction, but honestly, he didn't have the need. Jumping, I tackled Ramses myself, jabbing him over and over again in the side even if I didn't put much force in it.

"Take. That. Back." I laughed, now giving him a noogie which probably looked fucking hilarious considering his size versus mine. I messed up his hair and everything, and chuckling, he grabbed my hands.

"Get her off me, Prinze," Ramses urged, but Royal simply stood there.

He braced his arms over his chest. He'd worn a suit under that graduation cap and gown, looking fine as hell. He grinned. "I mean, if she wants to keep putting her hands on you, who am I to stop her?"

Ramses frowned, wresting my arms behind my back. "Bastard."

The humor left Royal's green eyes, but I worked my arms out and got between the boys. I firmly believed they'd *still* kill each other even after all we'd been through, but gratefully, Royal's boys backed me up.

"All right. All right. Party's over," LJ stated, joining us on the balcony. The tall blond cleaned up too, and though his suit wasn't as fancy as Royal's or even Ramses's, he still looked good. All the Court boys did, Jax with his buzzed hair and Knight behind him. The flurry of boys crowded this small overlook that gave views of Windsor House's gardens and man-made lake.

Knight leaned back against the banister. "I say let them fight. My money is on Mallick."

Royal shot him a look. "What the fuck?"

Knight raised a shoulder, grinning. "What? The mother-fucker's squirrelly. Let's see what he's got."

Royal lifted blond eyebrows before easing me away from Ramses. He took Ramses's place in the end, being all posses-sive and caveman-like when he snaked his arm around my waist. "Need I remind you all I kicked the dude's ass before?"

Ramses barked a laugh. "Hardly. I gave you that black eye, bro."

"Want to try it again?" Royal growled, but came back when I jerked him.

I placed a hand on his chest. "No one is kicking anyone's ass unless it's Jax's for that tie," I said, pointing at Jax. Dude actually had Snoopy on it.

Jax smoothed his tie down. "Okay, I sense some discrimi-nation here, so I'm just going to bow out of here."

But the boys didn't let him, all of them tackling him. Even Ramses. A dude circle mock-pounded on each other with me in the middle, but I didn't bother stopping it this time. I got too much joy seeing those who used to be enemies come together again. If only Paige could see.

Eventually, they did break it up, and *eventually,* I got one of my best friends and my boyfriend at opposite corners. The party wasn't nearly as lively after that but still fun. I stayed to the end, and even my dad and Aunt Celeste stayed for most of the graduation party too.

I got a hug from them both, Rosanna as well because she came. Dad made me promise to come home at a decent time because he had a graduation present for me when I got there. He decided not to sell the house after all, since things seemed better and Aunt Celeste was even making a permanent switch to come out and live with us. We'd all be under the same roof since I decided to stay there too while going to community college in the fall.

"Any idea what my dad's gift might be?" I asked Royal

later that night. We didn't need to stay and clean up. Obviously, Windsor House had staff for that, but the pair of us did. I think it helped us both mellow down.

Royal trashed a red Solo cup, his lips twisted in a grin. "What makes you think I'd know anything about that?"

Approaching, I snaked my arms around his waist. I shrugged. "I don't know, because I've been seeing you two whispering about something."

Like seriously, all the damn time now. I even caught them watching sports together on Monday nights. WTF.

Dropping his trash, Royal brought big arms around me. "Well, it's supposed to be a surprise."

"And it's clearly not now. So..."

He touched his mouth to mine, smiling. "It's a ski trip. To my family's cabin, which is why he brought me in on it. I'm loaning it to him for use. He invited me to go too."

"Well, that was really nice of you."

"It's the least I could do, right? I mean, he might not have any daughters if it wasn't for me."

He said that very seriously, and that saddened me. He was still taking responsibility for things that weren't his fault.

"You're going to promise me something, okay?" I stated, lacing our fingers together. "You're not going to punish yourself for things you have no control over anymore. It's not healthy."

And could be the very thing that may get in between us. He'd have no more room for anyone else, least of all me if he couldn't handle his guilt.

Sitting down on a folding chair, Royal took me with him, staring up at me with those beautiful eyes. I'd never get over seeing myself in them, all that warmth, all that love. He hugged me tight. "I love you, Em. I love you always."

Like everything else he said, I knew he meant that too.

I brought my arms around him. "I love you always."

We'd need that, both of us. We'd have a long way to go for

healing after all this, and when he was weak, I'd be strong and vice versa. We'd be each other's rocks.

Silently, I thanked my sister for something else, letting him kiss me and sinking into it. I never would have found him if it wasn't for her.

I just wished she could have been here to see it.

EPILOGUE

Two Years Later

Royal

"Why does it look like these floors aren't vacuumed?"

December and I gazed up from the box of her stuff we'd been unpacking. How in fuck's sake a girl had so much shit I had no idea, but I'd moved at least three suitcases of her stuff up three fucking flights of stairs.

God only knows how my girlfriend decided to pick a college dorm without a damn elevator.

That'd been her choice, though, and I went with it as with most things when it came to her. I'd really become nothing but a pushover, but I couldn't help it. I enjoyed making her happy, but who was *not* happy was Mr. Lindquist who currently stressed the fuck out about the state of her dorm room floors. He currently paced over the hardwood, his hand in his pocket.

He tugged his phone out with a frown. "I'm going to make a call. This is unacceptable. How do they expect kids to get off to a good start if their rooms are filthy?"

I, particularly, wouldn't consider one of the top schools in the state filthy, but to each his own.

And Em thought *I* was anal.

I just liked my stuff a certain way, and sighing, December got up from her new bed and wiggled her little ass over to her dad by the door. Reaching back into her suitcase to pull out more stuff, I tried to keep it from being obvious I was checking out the goods in front of her dad.

But oh, would I be hitting that later.

Especially after the little surprise I planned to tell her after her dad and aunt finally left us. Good luck ever getting a moment alone with my girlfriend when I came back into town. I'd been flying private jets for a little over a year now, working mostly for the government. The hardest part had been the clearances once I got out of flight school. I'd been flying since I was sixteen and had no problems with my certifications.

So much had changed, more time away from my girlfriend than I would've liked. I didn't get to see her a lot since I'd been working so much, but all that was about to change...

That was if I could get her alone.

"Dad, it's fine," she stressed, pleading with Mr. Lindquist with that little pout thing she did. It never ceased to work its magic on me. She frowned hard. "I brought a vacuum. I can take care of it."

Clearly unsatisfied with that, Mr. Lindquist started dialing, and beside him was December's aunt Celeste. Together, niece and aunt rolled their eyes, and when Celeste passed me a wink, I knew she was about to do me a solid and get Mr. Lindquist the hell out of here. We'd talked about this, and she knew my plans for December's surprise.

Celeste placed her hands on Mr. Lindquist's shoulders,

directing him out of the room. "Come on, Rowan. Let's go talk to the administration. I'm sure they could help with the issue."

Celeste had always been on my team, and it'd been her to actually get Mr. Lindquist to kind of like me over the years. She'd officially moved to Maywood Heights the summer of December's and my graduation and had a nice place next door to Mr. Lindquist's. December and I always seemed to find our way over there while she'd been attending community college. Her aunt Celeste loved to cook and stuff.

"Good idea," Mr. Lindquist grumbled, huffing before bringing December over. Giving her a hug, he told her he'd straighten this out before leaving, and I'd never get over how close the two had gotten. Somewhere along the way with everything that happened with Paige, Mr. Lindquist had turned into the father Paige had always wished she had. I was happy at least December got to have that. We didn't all have great dads, and I hadn't seen mine since his ass went off to prison. That day he'd finally admitted to what he'd done to my best friend, he'd died, and as far as I was concerned, I was an orphan. I liked it that way, all I already had in my life more than enough.

Popping up, I grabbed December by the hips, making her squeal when I pulled her into me. We fell on her bed, and she was a sea of giggles, the sound nothing short of heaven to my ears. I could go to peaceful sleep with her voice and had so many times.

I twisted strands of hair so dark they nearly shined raven black, umber wisps I'd never get enough of touching.

"Reach into my pocket," I told her, snuggling up on her, and she eyed me.

"What will I find if I do?" she asked, her lips humming against mine, and I chuckled. She wouldn't find *that*, at least not now. Holding her close, I directed her to reach for the back one, and out of the pocket, she got a letter. I gave her some distance to read it, and I couldn't explain the feeling I got as I watched her expression change. It shifted from surprise, to joy, and then sheer elation.

"Are you serious?" she asked, and I nodded at her, totally serious. Her lips parted. "But you're flying… You *love* flying."

I did, but I wanted to be closer to her. That was the beauty of having money, the one good thing from my dad. I could do anything I wanted with my life, getting my degree amongst them.

I slid my acceptance letter to this very school out of her hand. "I wouldn't cramp your style being here?"

Perhaps she wanted more freedom, to have some time and enjoy school without the boyfriend hovering over her. I wouldn't love that, but I'd respect it. I'd give her anything, and sliding her arms around my neck, she pressed her lips to mine.

"I've missed you so much," she said, making that solid muscle in my chest start again. I thought it was dead for a long time, only fleeting beats of happiness here and there. It had gotten to the point where I only got it to work in the past when I'd been around Paige and the guys, and flying. But since Em came into my life, I couldn't seem to make it *not* start beating.

"We get to go to college together? Really?" she asked me. She transferred here to start her junior year, and though I'd be coming in as a freshman, we would be going to school together. I planned to max out my course load each semester as well as take summer classes and could easily shave off a year as long as I worked hard. I had no problem doing that.

"We do," I said, another surprise I planned to share with her soon. She thought she couldn't bring her dog Hershey to college with her, the pup staying home with her dad. But not only had I already secured my own place, her dad gave me permission to have Hershey come stay with me so she'd be closer to December. Of course, as long as December didn't mind that. I hugged her. "And we can have more too if you want that."

Her eyes widened. "What do you mean?"

"I mean, I'm going to fucking marry you." I grabbed her, making her giggle again. "And the where and when will be a lot easier if we're in the same hemisphere."

I'd flown all around the world for my job, had so many experiences already and in such little time. But one experience I really wanted was back home.

"Please, dear God, tell me that wasn't your proposal," she teased, and I shifted her on her back.

"Oh, you'll get that later." I mouthed the words against her neck, making her sigh. "Don't you worry about that."

In fact, the guys had flown in today just for it. Everyone but Knight since he actually already went to school at this university. The other two, Jax and LJ had been in other parts of the country pursuing their various educations, but when I'd asked them all to be here for a special proposal, they'd dropped everything they were doing. Knight, Jax, and LJ were no doubt stuffing their faces somewhere in the college cafeteria, on standby for our dinner tonight. I'd planned a big one and even gotten her dad's permission with the caveat we wouldn't actually tie the knot until she finished school. He was level-headed like that, and I'd have given him anything he wanted to have his daughter. I had a feeling though my girl may be the one in the end to fight that agreement once she found out about it. We'd see.

I had a lot of losses in my life, so many in fact, and if I wanted something, I refused to not take it. Life could be fleeting, the moments the same, but what wasn't was my love for this girl and her sister. Between December and me, Paige would always live on. She'd always be there and never would be forgotten because of me, because of December. I didn't do the forgetting thing anymore.

If I did, my girl would hand me my ass and then some.

Dear reader,

Thank you so much for checking out the Court High series! You guys are all truly amazing for taking a chance on a new to you author and I can't thank you enough!!!

What's next for Royal, December, and the rest of the folks from Maywood Heights you may ask? Well, I'm happy to let you know there are so many more books for you to sink your teeth into in the Court world! Royal and Em's story may be done, *for now*, but their friends Knight, LJ, Jax, and Ramses all have stories available for download today! Start with book one in the Court University series, Brutal Heir, today! (More details on the next page!)

Love y'all,

Eden

Brutal Heir (Court University #1)

Never trust a campus god.

Knight Reed is a devil heir with a chip on his shoulder. The arrogant a-hole I love to hate.

His name may be Knight, but that armor is black as coal. He's a beautiful god with a wicked heart. I know because my mom used to work for his family. An act of brutal violence in the woods and he gets my mom fired, ultimately leaving us homeless. That was the last time I saw him face-to-face.

At least, until recently.

He's frat boy royalty at my new university, a campus god amongst the rich and elite. There's little interest in a freshman like me.

But then I cross him, putting an end to me being invisible here in his world.

At a party, I see something I shouldn't have seen. Now, suddenly, the campus god has me tackled on a bed with his hand around my throat. He tells me to forget what I witnessed. Do that or the end result will be bad for me. He's hellbent on crushing my little dove wings and all I see is that cruel boy from the woods that day.

When it comes to Knight, I can't seem to stay out of his way or keep my trap shut around him, no matter how hard I try. He tells me my little mouth will get me in trouble, but I think he's wrong.

I'm not afraid what will happen if I spill his secrets. What terrifies me is how badly I want to see what might be beyond all that coal-black armor...

It's possible that, to some small measure, I'm tempted to give in to the only devil I've ever known.

The dark knight himself.

Did you know there's a website dedicated to all things Court High? There is and it features exclusive content you can't get anywhere else! The website exclusives include playlists, graphics, character bios/photos, and so much more!

Want access to the website? Simply subscribe to my newsletter! There, you'll get new release news from me and a link to the newsletter exclusive Court High website. What are you waiting for? Get access today! =^)

Website access: https://bit.ly/3v7nTu5

13238475R00129